MADEMOISELLE

BENOIR

✤   ✤   ✤

MADEMOISELLE

BENOIR

CHRISTINE

CONRAD

HOUGHTON MIFFLIN COMPANY

BOSTON • NEW YORK

2006

1-2006

For information about permission to reproduce selections from
this book, write to Permissions, Houghton Mifflin Company,
215 Park Avenue South, New York, New York 10003.

Visit our Web site: www.houghtonmifflinbooks.com.

Library of Congress Cataloging-in-Publication Data

Conrad, Christine.
Mademoiselle Benoir / Christine Conrad.
p.   cm.
ISBN-13: 978-0-618-57479-7
ISBN-10: 0-618-57479-4
1. Americans — France — Fiction. 2. Aristocracy
(Social class) — Fiction. 3. Middle-aged women — Fiction.
4. Lot (France) — Fiction. 5. Young men — Fiction.
6. Artists — Fiction. I. Title.
PS3603.O5553M33 2006 813'.6—dc22
                                2005012176

Printed in the United States of America

Book design by Robert Overholtzer

QUM 10 9 8 7 6 5 4 3 2 1

This is a work of fiction. Although many of the
settings are real, some are imagined.

FOR J.R., K.B., P.S., AND K.M.

Love is a dwelling where being there is enough.

— WALLACE STEVENS

MADEMOISELLE

BENOIR

✣   ✣   ✣

APRIL 1998

Mas La Viguerie

Dear Mom and Dad,

I am writing to you sitting at the window of my new house! Since I moved in on Sunday, there have been brilliant sun showers, blazing rainbows, thick curtains of rain hanging at the horizon, and all manner of spectacular cloud effects. Absolutely jaw-dropping.

Sorry you've had so little news, but the last four months have been hell. For a while it looked as if the deal to buy the property was dead in the water, and I had all but given up. After I put down the ten percent earnest money and signed the *promesse de vente,* the next step was to get all seven heirs to the property to sign off on the deal. A M. Hector Aubrac, living in Paris and doing God-knows-what, was the last holdout. Maître Lussac, the notary handling the negotiations, kept writing to this elusive relative but got no reply. Finally, he asked me for money in order to travel to Paris to nail down this last signature. His ploy was to make a threat regarding unpaid inheritance taxes on the property.

Needless to say, I've learned a lot more than I wanted to about French inheritance laws. They seem to be unbelievably archaic. Unlike in America, you can't leave your property to anyone you want; three quarters must go to your children. The end result is that magnificent properties fall slowly to ruin as the heirs squabble over how to divide or take care of them.

So the stress got really unbearable. Uncertainty is definitely a lot worse in a culture not your own. Janie's place had served its purpose for the last year, and I loved Villefranche de Rouergue — it's quite a lively town — but her house was right in the center, on a dark street, cramped, with little light during the day, and I had no real study, so I was very anxious to move. Janie was incredibly sweet, but then things got very sticky. When we were in graduate school together, I thought she was so sophisticated. She had lived in Paris with her parents, her dad was a diplomat, she spoke French fluently, etc., etc. After Maurice the actor-boyfriend moved out on her last month, she began coming over to my side of the house every night, just to talk, she claimed. It was as if a puddle appeared at my door every night. I really don't understand why she came to live here in the first place. No doubt some very romantic, but delusional idea. Okay, okay, I know what you're thinking, but in my case I think my motivation to move here was verrrry solid.

From the first moment I saw this property, I had a bead on it. I can't completely explain why, but I had an intense feeling of belonging.

You enter the *mas* by a narrow road with thick brush on both sides that goes for quite a run, and then a quick turn to the right and, *voilà:* the house in its proud but battered glory. It isn't a large farmhouse, but it has beautiful cone-shaped slate turrets and plenty of room to expand. The barn has "studio" written all over it.

After the house was *finally* deeded over to me, I had to start to make it livable immediately. A new roof was put on first. I stole the tiles for it from the sheep barn, thereby leaving it completely roofless, which I'll worry about if and when I ever get some sheep. I put in a new well for catching rain and source water, a generator for electricity, and a septic tank. These improvements have turned out to cost a lot more than I thought they would, but I wanted to get it all done at once. Getting a really decent bathtub is a bit away, but now there is at least a good strong shower, although the bathroom is still pretty primitive.

Cleaning out the main house proved to be particularly backbreaking, but I got some help from Gaspar, who is the son of a neighbor. He is slightly retarded but a sweet soul, and as strong as an ox. He was thrilled with his new job. We dragged out old, dead mattresses, piles of broken furniture, and then we whitewashed all the walls. There

3

was almost nothing worth keeping, except an old armoire that I plan to refinish. Mostly there was just broken crockery, but I managed to salvage a few pieces that looked as if they might have some value. Also, Janie gave me some stuff from the house in Villefranche, not much, a buffet, some lamps, etc. I also went to the *brocante* in Cajarc and picked up lots of stuff, a pair of dynamite candlesticks, a whole bunch of assorted dishes and cutlery for the kitchen.

So I now live in the country of France, region of Quercy, department of Lot, city of Cajarc, commune of St.-Jean d'Olt. France is so *orderly* — a big surprise — not what I expected at all, given some very uninformed notions concerning the French reputation for passion and sensuality. And boy, do these people love "forms," a form for this, a form for that, I must have filled out dozens.

In any case, my commune of St.-Jean d'Olt has sixty-four official inhabitants, but I think that includes M. Meyrac's three goats. And this is not counting the ghosts of thousands of years who still make their presence felt. The imprint of the past is so strong here that some days I feel as if I can actually see men and women of centuries ago, standing at the stone water troughs or drawing water from the stone wells.

Many people find the Lot Valley desolate, but for me it has a very human scale. The landscape unfolds bend by bend, layer upon layer, field by field, gorge by gorge. The stones and trees show marks of habitation since the be ginning of mankind. Goths, Vikings, Romans, Celts, you name it. This place just naturally pushes you to see the bigger picture because here time has both stood still . . . and moved on.

You may think of my living here as isolated and lonely, but I don't experience it that way at all. At least not right now. I know I will have such periods and I have to steel myself for them, but I'm still enthralled by this place.

Your son,
Tim

Marjorie Reinhart,
280 West 73d Street, New York

Dear Tim,

I have to be honest, when you first left the city, I was sure you wouldn't last more than six months in France. So when I read your letter today about buying the farm, my heart stopped beating. Because buying the farm says that *you really mean it;* you're going to stay there for a long time. True, you were much more given to solitude than your sister, who still can't stand to be alone for a minute, but how did you manage to pick the most remote and underpopulated part of France? Why not Paris at least? Have you forsworn all culture? Excuse me for being crass, but all that expensive schooling doesn't count for much in that part of the world. What are your choices? Farmer? Blacksmith? Shepherd? You were an assistant professor of mathematics, for God's sake, and by now you could easily be an associate . . . could be . . . could be . . . Is this what you really had in mind for your life? It seems so final and not the sort of move that you can reverse very easily.

Right now you are riding the high of buying the farm, but what about a year from now? Do you really want to live on such a pittance? Life is very expensive, travel especially. I hope you have taken into consideration the fact that you could be completely tied down there because you can't afford to go anywhere.

Please forgive the mother's lament, but the news has hit me very hard. So. Anyway. Moving on to some neutral housekeeping stuff: I have sent you the papers you asked for from the storage boxes. I also included a bag of goodies, just some crackers and nonperishable stuff — you can't keep a mother down. Other news from here: Your sister and Brad seem to be doing better after a rocky first year of married life. They were living in that extremely cramped apartment in SoHo, which exacerbated all their tensions, and now have found something at least more livable in Park Slope. But it is clearly human nature not to leave well enough alone for a single minute, and they are now trying to get pregnant. So when a baby arrives, the new place will be too small!

I ran into Kristen the other day. She still seems to be pining away for you, or is this just my imagination? She peppered me with questions about your life in France.

Love,
Mom

Mas La Viguerie

Dear Mom,

I know that despite your own nonconformism, you and Dad find the same qualities unsettling in an offspring. I also know what Gram thought about you when you went to Paris at age twenty-two and lived what Gram called "that pretend Bohemian life." I'd like to see the letters she wrote to *you*. Need I say more?

Let's face it, I was not doing well at American life. You educated me to think for myself, so that's what I'm doing. I turn thirty-four this year, so it's now or never. Maybe you and Dad should take some of the blame — after all, you conditioned me for a cultural world that hardly exists anymore. The America you brought me into was a very different place from what it is now. I think you naively expected that "culture" — your kind of high-minded culture — would win out, cream rising to the top. But what you didn't count on was the dumbing-down-of-America factor. So instead, you have become — if you pardon my saying so — an anachronism, stuck with complaining about the barrage of crap on TV and how Americans have become moronic cartoon versions of themselves because of the constantly perpetuated images in the media. How "information pollution" — Dad's favorite lament — doesn't represent knowledge of any kind, and so on. I love theoretical mathematics, and I loved teaching it, but I couldn't handle the politics of academic life. I have a low tolerance for the bullshit. When it comes to doing your work, it's difficult just to *do the work*. You have to do work that is "acceptable." Otherwise you can't get grants to support your work.

But more than anything, I wanted to get off the American treadmill of success with a capital S and shut off the relentless background noise. No cell phones, no constant demands from everywhere in the culture to buy this, buy that, buy anything. I'd like to think of myself as something more than an open mouth with a credit card. I read yesterday that a group of scientists has asked that use of the Internet be limited among them because it's interfering with their ability to think. I couldn't agree more. I'd like to devote more energy to thinking about what I was put on this earth for, and I want to do the simple things: work hard, perfect my craft. As the Buddhists say, Chop wood, carry water.

Forgive the long rant, but I mean it. I want an authentic life — or at least I want to find out if it's possible.

Your son,

Tim

Matt Reinhart,
280 West 73d Street, New York

Dear Tim,

Your mother seems to believe that if *I* write to you, you will be persuaded to her point of view. This has never worked in the past, and why should it? But I continue to play my part. As you also know, I am not a financier, just the opposite, so whatever I say about money, consider the source. But I did contact George the accountant, who says I'm to tell you to watch the currency fluctuations and try to squeeze out the best bang for your buck.

Please know that I have somehow managed to accumulate a few dollars and they are at your service if you need them. Of course, I won't let you get your hands on my vast millions. But let us know. We want to help out.

Frankly, I feel some envy, not for living in uncomfortable and damp places — God knows, I am way too old for that — but for, I don't know, the fuck-all quality of making such a move, I guess. If you don't like a place, hey, just pick up and get out. I don't happen to like feeling stuck anywhere either — never did in my working life. But I'm not sure I didn't pay a big price for it. Moving around from university to university, you get a mark. Ah well . . . In any case, it would be very difficult now to get your mother to leave the city, no matter how much she complains about it.

Dad

Mas La Viguerie

Dear Mom and Dad,

Dad, thanks for your generous offer, but I cannot accept. I need to maintain complete self-sufficiency and it is all too easy to slip into a habit of knowing there are always a few extra dollars one can rely on. I don't want that to happen. The line is drawn and even though it may be an imaginary line, I have to stay on this side of it.

And, Mom: please, please, stop the reflexive worrying. One of the unexpected pluses of my moving to France has been our ability to communicate in letters in a detached non-mother-son dynamic. Your novelist's thirst for details makes you the perfect person to write to, as you appreciate every nuance. I can't write these kinds of letters to anyone else I know! This is a deep compliment. But when your "mother anxiety" floods the system, I have to withdraw to protect myself. So please stop spoiling it!

As I've already told you, I can get by on very little here. There is Grandpa's legacy. Modest though it is, it keeps my boat afloat, even if it's only a rowboat. Unlike on Columbus Avenue — where a glass of wine is $9 (and rising) — I can have a glass at the local bar for about 50 cents. No more daily $15 cab fares. Money is put to the essentials of living. I am also eating very well, and very healthfully, thanks to a truck that appears in the village weekly with the freshest possible produce. No McDonald's here, no fast food at all, which was my weakness in

11

New York. After years of ambivalence, seesawing between math classes and art school, then making a real living teaching math, but always lusting after time to paint, I came here to see if I can become whole and find out if I really have the goods as an artist. One thing is for sure, I love doing it and my heart has always been more on the side of painting. While I work to set up a proper studio here and get ready for some serious painting, I have been doing lots of drawings. I have a two-pronged approach: I get my eye and hand geared up for bigger challenges, and at the same time I hope I can make extra money selling my drawings.

And please don't form the view that I am a hermit here. I think I actually felt much more isolated in that studio apartment on West 78th and Columbus. I would work intensely all day, and then go out for a walk at night and feel alone in a sea of people. In fact, I have the best of both possible worlds here. I can communicate with friends everywhere by phone or mail, but I am also living in this beautiful place. Besides, fighting isolation is not the worst thing in life. I used to see the old people sitting all day on the benches at Broadway and 72d, just waiting for their lives to end. You can live in a city of millions and be completely isolated from anything human.

Your son,
Tim

Holly Reinhart-Saxon,
Park Slope, Brooklyn

Dear Bro,

Ever since you dropped the news on the parents that you bought a farmhouse, Mom has not stopped vibrating and has been calling me nonstop. So congratulations on the house — and thanks a whole lot. When you decided to try living in France last year, I was your most fervent supporter, but is it really fair that I have to take on the whole familial load on this side of the Atlantic?

Never mind, just venting — if you're happy, I'm happy. I have to admit that I couldn't help thinking about what would have happened if I was the one who moved to France and was living alone in an ancient farmhouse. Our mother would have sent out a posse and I would have been carted back home and institutionalized.

When we were growing up, they told us that a boy child and a girl child were absolutely equal, and we were encouraged to follow our dreams. There was no limit to what we both could achieve. Which was all great at first, until it became clear to me — when I hit thirteen or so — that, wait a minute, it's not an equal society! It's a man's world. It's like when the games really begin, I'm wearing ankle weights and a sign that says, "Caution: woman inside."

Why am I brooding about this just now? Because having become a married woman, the baby decision is pressing down hard, so the "equality" thing has been eating at me. Brad wants baby, great, but Brad doesn't carry baby, Holly carries baby. Then Holly must find a way to work (which she loves) and take care of baby. Biology is clearly destiny. Sigh, sigh, sigh. But you'll be glad to know I don't hold you personally responsible in any way. What I really hate is that you're not here right now for one of our great debates.

Please send pictures of the new abode. I hope you've at least got indoor plumbing.

Love,
Holly

280 West 73d Street, New York

Dear Tim,

Guess what? Holly and Brad were here for dinner last night, and she announced that she is pregnant. Son-in-law was in a complete state and wants her to stop working immediately. He created quite a ruckus after I said I thought she should work as long as she feels like it. It's not easy to kick a son-in-law out of your house.

The other day I had lunch with my friend Ilsa Markey. Do you remember her daughter, Linda Markey? She was in your class at Ethical. Well, it seems Linda has married a Frenchman, who was working as an investment banker in Manhattan, but as soon as they married he insisted that they go back to France to live. Her mother says the poor girl didn't know what she was in for. She fantasized that living in Paris would be so glamorous and stimulating. But what she discovered was that upon entering the country she was instantly only the "daughter-in-law," with strictly prescribed duties. She and her husband spend every weekend at her mother-in-law's in the country, which is a three-hour drive from Paris. When there, she has no time for herself and is expected to cater to this charming but demanding woman. The Sunday lunch goes on for hours and hours. And no matter what she does, she is treated like an outsider — she's the "American wife." On this cheery note, I hope you have thought about what it means to be an expat. As long as you continue as you are, you can coast along, but what if you decide to marry a French girl? That's when you will realize that you are an outsider.

Your father has a chance to go to a meeting in Milan, and we thought we'd combine it with a trip to visit you. Hope you are agreeable to this?? Sometimes I think I absolutely need to see where you live, and other times I think it might be better left to my imagination.

But I am really looking forward to seeing you and seeing the Lot Valley. Provence we've been to; Paris many times; we've hit the châteaus in the Loire, but the Lot is a complete mystery. A woman I know visited last year and says she did not see another American tourist for the whole two weeks that they were there. Amazing.

But most of all I could really use some peace and quiet and some time away from my manuscript.

Your Mom

P.S. Heads-up: Kristen asked for your address.

Mas La Viguerie

Dear Mom,

I just got a funny note and drawing from Holly about getting pregnant. It shows her kicking and screaming, so she's obviously having a very hard time, but I know she's going to be a great mother.

So you think this place is quiet? I'm just beginning to adjust to the noise level here in the mornings. Cackling cicadas start very early, then the birds pick up the beat, then the various barnyard animals have to put their two cents in. Christ, it's almost as noisy as trucks barreling down Columbus Avenue at six A.M. But just as I did with city noise, I'm sure there will come a time when I don't notice it.

Updates from here: I recently met, or shall I say — *fait la connaissance de* — one of my neighbors. Her name is Marcelline Becaze and she works as a lawyer in Ville-franche de Rouergue. She was born in the Midi and her family lives about two hundred miles from here. We met in a nearby *commune,* where on Thursdays they sell their produce out of the back of a truck — unbelievably cheap and fresh. Yesterday I bought these delicious little round goat cheeses called *cabécou,* about the size of hockey pucks (I could become addicted), luscious-looking butter lettuce, green beans, a chicken, strawberries, two bottles of a local red wine, and I got the whole lot for the equivalent of fifteen bucks.

Marcelline is renting a small house about a mile from me. Since then, we have bought groceries for each other, and this week we're going shopping together to Cajarc for bigger stuff. She is very attractive in a dark, intense way. Age about thirty is my guess. She seems deeply French, although I'm not sure yet what I mean by this, but whatever it is I feel it strongly. I need to be here longer to know what deeply French really is. My sketching has made me aware of the various French faces, and I've begun to recognize types that probably go back, oh, say 2,500 years. When I was in Villefranche a few weeks ago, I sat next to a guy in a café who was right out of *The Three Musketeers*: thin hooked nose, angular face, goatee, an arrogant tilt to his chin. It was like looking at a painting from the seventeenth century. An American lives in a "melting pot," but in France there has been a relatively continuous cultural chain of thousands of years. I'm just beginning to sort out the difference in sensibilities that this longevity creates.

It's great — and I mean that absolutely — that you want to visit. I'm really looking forward to it. But to be comfortable, you might want to stay in a hotel in Cajarc, or in fact stay in *the* hotel in Cajarc, as I think there's only one. Let me know when you're coming and I will make arrangements.

As for marrying a French girl, I'll cross that bridge when I come to it.

Your son,
Tim

Brian Hedrick, Boston

Dear Timbo,

Sorry for taking so long to write back, but I've been up to my eyeballs in the new job and finding a new place to live. I had to let go of our old Cambridge apartment, which was getting way too college-boy for a thirty-four-year-old guy. (I threw out our old Blondie poster. I hope you can live with that.)

As you can imagine, McNamara and Co. is a real suit-and-tie deal. They actually offered to get me a "shopper," as they are obviously aware of the haberdashery deficiencies of their incoming mathematicians. Apparently we applied-math guys are in superdemand, and they are paying me lots of bucks. I'm going to give this mega-consulting two years, and then the plan is to go back to doing hard-ass original work.

You'll love this: In my meeting with the recruiter who hired me, I told him I wanted to work with nonprofits — I actually told the guy I wanted to make a difference. He looked at me as if I were the millionth poor jerk that he's had to disabuse of this idea. His answer was that if you "work with the right people your values will change. You're going to meet very attractive people and get to travel all over the world." But to be fair, we do get to do interesting stuff and I will be working with a lot of smart guys. Artie Simonson is going to be my immediate supervisor.

As for you, Timbo, I still can't believe you *actually* and *really* moved to France! I mean, we all fantasize about dropping through the net, getting off the treadmill, but I could never decide if that would be real courage or real self-destruction. And then for me, there was always the "Are there any girls there?" question.

But we've been through so much together, we're not going to lose touch, not if I can help it. There's a very good chance I'll be able to get over your way for a few weeks' vacation (another perk from McNamara). So get ready.

Brian

Mas La Viguerie

Dear Corporate Man,

Let's face it: between us, you had the superior math brain — and the hottest hand. You got onto K-theory long before it got really sexy. So congrats on the new gig, but I hope you keep current and don't lose your mojo. Two years can be a long time.

I have to say I loved "You will meet very attractive people and travel the world." Is the point of being alive to be distracted, to take a cruise ship through life? That's just what I don't want. I love to have fun — and lots of it — but I also need to take life seriously, not just putz around. Of course, a good argument against me would be that it's the lucky person to take a cruise ship through life. Does one really want the "real-life" experience of living through, say, a famine or a plague? But my point is that if you become inauthentic, I think in the end the price is extremely high.

But never mind. It's absolutely great that you're going to show up here. Biking is a must-do thing in these parts. Trips with our Cambridge bike club to Concord and Mount Wachusett were kid stuff compared to rides around the spectacular gorges here, so get yourself into some reasonable shape so that we can do some really hard riding. I can set you up with a good bike (or *vélo*, as they call it here), unless you want to be fanatic about it and bring your own wheels.

As for women here, you might be amazed at the number of blondes. They're called *blondes d'Aquitaine*. Big, beautiful, white, and slow-moving. Just your type. In fact there are about a hundred grazing in the next field over from mine.

Timbo

Mas La Viguerie

Dear Mom and Dad,

Marcelline thanks you for the book, Mom, and is superimpressed that I have a mother who is actually a published novelist. She is enchanted by her present and claims she's going to read every English word of it.

She and I are now spending a few evenings a week at my place, and it is very pleasant. On those evenings we cook together. Marcelline has the frugal ways of the French, and we manage to have delicious dinners for very little. Sometimes she brings stuff from her kitchen garden. Last night it was little white squashes, tomatoes, and fresh herbs. I am fascinated by all the food knowledge she takes for granted. She actually makes her own vinegar from a "mother" that her mother gave her. She claims it's extremely important to use a good wine when making vinegar, and she made me sniff the very expensive stuff I'd bought in Villefranche and then here, and the difference was amazing. I really believe my nose has come back from the dead. City living shuts down your nose (for good reason). She also makes her own peppermint tea (*tisane*), but she takes this for granted, too. It's what we did at home, she says. Why pay money just for the packaging in the market? And she has a Frenchwoman's inborn artistry. Everything she places on a table can take on an instant beauty, whereas whatever I do looks plunked-down. When I mentioned this, she was somewhat embarrassed and waved it off. I think she is divided in herself about growing up on a farm. As a lawyer, she is a "modern" woman, given to the mental, and she has a big resistance to being seen as a "farm girl." But the truth is I really love her farm-girl side, and I'm prodding her to help me put in a kitchen garden here.

Later in the evening, I work on the drawings I'm hoping to sell, and Marce works on her briefs. I have done loads of sketches of local scenery. I try to get in at least one good sketch a day, to build up a decent portfolio.

Because my French is still not at all perfect, we have some hilarious misunderstandings. Yesterday I thought I told her after dinner that I was full. *Je suis plein,* I said. Apparently, I told her I was pregnant. Another time I managed to mangle my French in such a way that she thought I said I was tired of her. I am trying to comprehend some of her "issues" — as they would say in the States — and I am learning certain unspoken rules of French life. Marcelline has tipped me off, for example, on *boulangerie* etiquette. If I first say "*Bonjour, madame,*" and then ask for bread, I get treated very well. Just asking straight out for a loaf of bread was getting me cold stares. These people put a lot of stock in politeness and they have their rules.

Today I made a resolution to read Pascal, something I'm sure you'd approve of, Dad. I recently found out that he was born in Clermont-Ferrand, which is northeast of here, in the Rhône Valley, and this piqued my interest. All

I remember about Pascal from college was the time my math buddies latched onto his famous wager relating to God's existence. They got off on disproving it in several drunken sessions, but I must have been far away in my interests at the time and I tuned out.

I'd like to immerse myself in the background of the period before I get to Pascal's religious beliefs and mathematical proofs thereof. I gather that Pascal's famous *Pensées* were mostly notes, not completely polished ideas. Living in France gives me more of an impulse to reserve judgment; and God knows I have lots of unpolished writings of my own lying all over the place. People are still arguing over his stuff hundreds of years later, so no question the guy had a major impact. Given my own advanced age, the most scary thing I've learned about Pascal is that he died at thirty-nine.

Not *exactly* for this reason, I have begun hiking every day, in preparation for a long bike trip with Brian when he arrives. Brian finally gave up our old grungy apartment in Cambridge and has been seduced by the big bucks of a prestigious corporate consulting firm — something he vowed he would never do — so I can't wait to get a look at him in his new incarnation. I want to talk him into taking the traditional route of the religious pilgrims (the first "tourists" traipsing across France), starting from Villefranche and ending in Santiago de Compostela in Spain. But I think we'll have to compromise, as

Brian may have his heart set on meeting babes on the Côte d'Azur.

Your son,
Tim

Mas La Viguerie

Dear Kristen,

Princess, what a great surprise to hear from you! I've read your letter over so many times that there are sweaty palm prints all over the paper. So much came back to me — how much has changed — but *you* came back in blazing color. I won't elaborate, though, as the mail may be censored. You talk about how the city is becoming unlivable for you, but do you really think you could live here? I'm not sure you could hack it, despite your claim of wanting to strip your life down to the essentials.

Here is what my day is like: I get up at six, make my breakfast, which consists of yesterday's bread, toasted, a piece of chocolate, and coffee. Then I work for two to three hours on my drawings. Or I procrastinate for two or three hours on my drawings, whichever comes first.

Then I do hard physical labor outdoors for at least two hours. Yesterday, I cleared out an area behind my house, pulling up stone after stone after stone. This is a land of stones! I worked up a fierce sweat, and then I took a shower in my new but still primitive bathroom. A few times a week I bicycle into Cajarc for lunch. Most days, unless he's on a trip, my lunch companion is Paul, who runs a boat service on the Lot. This part of France is veined with beautiful rivers, and Paul has been a boatman all his life — as was his father before him, and who knows how many generations back. It's become a ritual for me to sit with him in a café and listen to his stories about the war. During WWII, Paul, eighteen years old, was shipped off by the Nazis to work in a creosote factory in Germany, and he was there for three years. When the war ended, he had to work in Paris as an elevator operator until he could get enough money to come home. I find all his stories about the war years just stunning. We have been so lucky in our lives.

Then when I get back to the house after lunch, every day without fail Chicken Lady is standing at my gate. She's Chicken Lady because when I pass her house, about a quarter mile from mine, she is always in the courtyard feeding the chickens. I can't quite tell how old she is, as she is slightly hunched over, which probably makes her seem much older. She shows up every day with something new for me. Today it was two eggs wrapped in newspaper — still hot from the chicken's butt. About a week ago, I was working on my gate and she suddenly lurched over and blurted out that she was in love with me. I didn't know what to say to this poor woman, so I just stared and she scurried away. She stayed away for about a week, but now she is back as if nothing has happened. She brought an offering of blackberries, and I wanted to say no, but the berries look so delicious (soaking the paper purple) I couldn't resist them. I think I have seen her looking into my windows, but I'm not positive. I know she is harmless, but it is still disconcerting.

So, these are my everyday friends. Not *your* usual social mix. Would you be delighted with all of this? Of course, but the question is, For how long?

Do I have a girlfriend? you ask. Well, there is a woman whom I spend time with. Actually she's a neighbor. She works as a lawyer in the market town of Villefranche de Rouergue. We started helping each other. But please, I don't want to go on about this. I would love to see you. You are absolutely welcome to come for a visit.

Love,
Tim

Mas La Viguerie

Dear Mom,

Well, Kristen just left, having lasted exactly two weeks. The first week was really great. I got quite caught up. Marcelline, by the way, stayed away. She was very cool about it — but maybe just very intuitive — or she didn't perceive a threat, or, I don't know. Frankly, I still can't read her very well. But why did I feel so guilty because Kristen came? What would a Frenchman have felt? Did I feel more guilty because I'm an American?

But never mind all that. Back to Kristen: On entering the house — and immediately realizing it is essentially one large room — her eyes quickly telegraphed, Oh God, is this really where I'm staying, what do I say, is *that* the bathroom, is *that* the kitchen, look at the floors, oh God, what do I say? She finally said: *I love it!*

But then we had a lot of fun. Kristen bounced off everything, and she is of course very, very bright. She was *fascinated* by the smallest thing. She read guidebooks, wrote in her diary, took pictures. In short, she *ran* through the place at breakneck speed.

I took her to see dolmens in the Causse de Limogne, which has a huge number of them. Needless to say, she was fascinated yet again and I was pretty fascinated myself. This part of the world has powerful remains of paganism. The stone dolmens are about fifteen feet high, sunbaked and covered with lichen and moss, and they have tilted dramatically over time. They were placed by people who lived here at least 10,000 years ago, before the Celts came to France. I read in the guidebook that the granite is not from this region, that the stones were actually transported, probably from northern Europe. As with the pyramids of Egypt, no one knows how. Incredible. I don't want to get too interested in them. Knowing myself, I could get completely obsessed and spend a lifetime trying to figure them out.

On the first weekend, I took Kristen on a boat ride on the Lot. Paul, my boatman friend, picked out the most spectacular part of the river for this trip, from St.-Cirq Lapopie to Bouzies, where we passed the magnificent Château des Anglais, used in the Hundred Years Wars. I was afraid that Paul was going to get us killed, as he never took his eyes off Kristen. He kept saying to me: *Tim, elle est incroyable. Elle reste longtemps, non?*

A hilarious moment came on Kristen's second day, when her cell phone screeched out on the *causse*. Here we are, surrounded by gorgeous juniper and oak trees, with sweeping vistas for miles, etc. At the sound of the phone, the sheep grazing on the next hill over actually pricked up their ears, or so I thought. Kristen was all "sheepish" and apologetic, but she still took the call! Talked on and on with her friend Carrie about Carrie's brand-new car, where she was going to garage it, etc., etc., and then it was on to the next topic.

By day five, Kristen was checking the guidebooks for restaurants for the evening. Let's go here, let's go there. I explained to her that unlike New Yorkers on the West Side of Manhattan, people here don't eat out *every night,* or otherwise get takeout.

And then the little fights began. Kristen enjoyed making wry comments about her antique accommodations. It was amusing at first, but then, whatever she did in the house, she had to get cute about its antiqueness. It began to get extremely irritating. What I came to realize is that Kristen's identity is completely tied up in what she *has,* her *things,* and her belief that they create a perception of her importance in the world. If these things suddenly disappear, she feels vulnerable and unimportant. Here she got zero reinforcement. God knows she is not alone in this, and God knows this is in part why I left the United States, but I never had the distance to see it until now. I was so tangled up with her physically and emotionally. And in truth I still think she is *au fond* a good woman and capable of more depth, but will she pull herself out of it? After she left, I sat outside in my garden for a long time and chewed over the fact that as time passes, the gap between me and my old friends in New York will probably get wider and wider. And so the world turns.

Your son,
Tim

P.S. I just got a set of wheels. Bought a *deux-chevaux* — do you remember them? — from a neighbor, for a very good price. Plus he said he'd do any mechanical work for me. I hope that doesn't mean I'll be fixing it all the time.

280 West 73d Street, New York

Dear Tim,

Your father can't believe that there is still a *deux-chevaux* in circulation. We actually rented one for a trip to the Loire Valley, and for me it was like driving around in a tin can for a week.

I am working seriously on detachment. The anxious mother, as you have eloquently pointed out, can be very unbecoming, not to mention counterproductive, and I believe I'm getting better. I'll never be a complete Buddhist, but your letter about Kristen was a big help. I like to think that I pay attention to people, but I realize I paid no attention to her, that is, to what she was *really* like, or why there should be a connection between the two of you. I think I was caught up in the picture-perfect element of you both. I admit that there was a time when I fantasized about a wedding. In some ways, I think I just wanted to wrap it up, get the whole marriage thing settled. A parent wants her child to land safely. Whatever our own experience, we have trouble letting you just float out into the universe.

I've never told you this, but your father seemed the most unlikely partner for me when we first got together. I was the "bohemian rebel." After college I went to work in Paris as a free-lance journalist, meaning that I had no job and hoped to send back stories to a friend at the *New York Times,* who got fired just as I arrived there. Then I lived "out of wedlock" with a French composer, very avant-garde (what other kind was there in France?). This was so horribly shocking in those years that your grandmother never got over it. She actually threw it up to me on her deathbed as the greatest disappointment of her life. At first glance, your father seemed too conventional for me. He was a serious academic, with very substantial papers on European history under his belt at an early age. He even smoked a pipe, for God's sake — men actually did that nasty thing in those days. His family was horrified: *She's a writer? Who actually lived in Paris, by herself?* You probably can't imagine all this now because we have achieved maximum "couplehood." We are now Marjorie-andMatt, a.k.a. the Reinharts. I see this same merging of identities among our close friends, at least the ones who never divorced! So I've decided that meddling does no good. When it comes to forming relationships, there can be deep connections between people that those on the outside may not see at first or understand. Therefore I've come to the not completely welcome realization that whom you decide to spend your life with is entirely up to you. *Voilà.*

Love,
Mom

Mas La Viguerie

Dear Mom and Dad,

Wow, Mom, how about dropping the novel and writing a memoir? We'd all like to hear about those wild and crazy Paris days.

It's certainly not wild and crazy here, at least in the Paris sense, but it sure is entertaining. On Saturday, Marcelline invited me to go with her to a lunch at a nearby farm in celebration of a haying. The owners of the farm, M. and Mme. Desaillac, are distant relatives of hers (I think she also does some legal work for them), and she said that I shouldn't miss this opportunity. The traditional celebration after a harvest is disappearing from French life as farms become more and more mechanized. She didn't have to twist my arm, and so off we went to the Desaillac farm, one of the largest around and about two miles from me. Long trestle tables were set up in the courtyard and filled with farm workers, neighbors, and family — about thirty-five souls in all. Looking like tired and hungry sentinels, the big tractors that had done the heavy lifting stood by the barn watching over the proceedings.

An incredible feast was laid out and just kept coming and coming in delicious waves. First there was a carrot soup, so wonderful that I was finished with it before everyone else at the table. Then I noticed that all those around me were putting a spoonful of wine into the remains of soup and then drinking from the bowl. It was explained to me that this very old tradition is called *le chabrot*, but unfortunately I didn't get the whole taste benefit, as I had nothing left in my bowl. And I thought you told me never to drink from my soup plate!

The feast continued: four different pâtés, bowls of fresh peas, bowls of stewed squash, legs of lamb, and roasted rabbits in mustard sauce — a first for me! Bottles of a delicious dark red wine were at every station. And then came the desserts: first fruit and cheese, then *clafouti*, a pudding-like concoction with cherries, which was unbelievably delicious, then an almond cake, a chocolate cake. I had to have a taste of every single thing. The amazing thing is that even though I thought I had eaten a ton of food, I didn't feel the least bit full afterward. What is it? The quality of the food, the freshness and purity? Anyway, it was a great experience.

Marce kept smiling over at me, watching me take the whole scene in. At some point, there was a rather tense conversation about the local *marginaux*. This is what they call "transients" in this part of the world — the equivalent of sixties hippies in Topanga Canyon. The *marginaux* have little money, live off crafts of some kind, and usually have a local relative who lets them stay for free in some abandoned house. Apparently there are more and more of them invading the valley. There was a half-joking moment at the table about whether I was a *marginal*. One of the men posed the question: Is it possible to be both a *marginal* and a foreigner. Obviously the locals have been spending a lot of time debating about how to categorize me. It was a good thing I had had a lot of wine because I could have gotten really tense and paranoid. Here everyone knows your business and, being an ex–city boy, I'm not at all used to it.

As the *eau de vie* (produced at the Desaillac farm) was passed around with the coffee, the men started to tease Marcelline. One of them proposed to her very drunkenly. He kept saying, Why isn't she married, she's so beautiful, what beautiful children they would make together, don't wait too long or you'll be an old maid. Mme. Desaillac kept sneaking glances at me, but as I said I had had quite a bit of the wine by this time and so I found it all quite affectionate and funny.

On the walk back to my place, Marce was furious. It was a gorgeous night, with moonlight flashing on the lichen-covered stone walls. I wanted to soak in the beauty, but she was so tense I thought she was going to crack in half. It was not funny, she kept repeating, *Les salauds, les idiots.* She is not someone who can brush these moments off easily. I told her that she should be flattered. All the men thought she was very beautiful. She laughed and rolled her eyes. Oh please, she said. It took me awhile to cajole her out of her mood, but then, whammo, she was full of energy and fun. Her mood swings keep me on my toes.

Tim

Mas La Viguerie

Dear Mom and Dad,

I had a very interesting dustup with a neighbor yesterday. I had decided to rebuild a section of the stone wall on the river side of the property. It's not the most compelling thing that needs to be done here, but every time I walk to the river I notice the large collapsed section. And it's also a very specific project, just a matter of lugging stones and then placing them on the wall. So I became compulsive and had to do it right away.

I spent the morning lugging stones — which is incredibly backbreaking work — almost like sitting at a computer all day, ha, ha. By five P.M., I was about two-thirds finished with the section I was working on, sweat was pouring off me, but I was feeling very virtuous, ready to quit and have a big glass of wine, when monsieur appeared. He was standing in the road on the other side of the wall, waving his arms frantically.

At first I couldn't understand what he was going on about, as his Midi dialect is very thick. He kept pointing to the wall. The only thing I could think of was that he was complaining about my workmanship — this is, after all, the first wall I've ever had anything to do with — and I was humble in the face of its long history. I said I'm sorry, monsieur, but I don't understand you. He just kept screaming and throwing his arms, and finally I headed back to the house. As I got into the house I could hear him still screaming in the road, but what could I do?

Well, I found out fast what his beef was: Apparently M. Carnac has been taking his sheep through my land, has been doing it for years, something no one mentioned to me and I had no way of knowing. Since it is now my land, I was under the impression that I could do anything I want with it, like repair my own stone wall. But not so fast. There are all kinds of French laws, written and unwritten: hunting rights, *droit du seigneur* stuff, preserving an "ancient right of way." The next day monsieur filed a lawsuit against me, claiming I am interfering with his business. If he had just been more patient and had tried to find a way to explain the problem, I'm sure we could have worked something out, but unfortunately now he's really pissed me off.

Well, it's nothing like a bit of trouble to learn pretty fast who runs the town. I complained to Maître Lussac, the *notaire* who handled the sale, and he was oh so apologetic, oh so polite. "*Monsieur, je suis désolé,* I had no idea, blah, blah, blah." When I went to see the former owner, he just shrugged and then said I didn't have to do anything if I didn't want to. Besides, M. Carnac files lawsuits every day. Don't pay any attention. Big help there. So then I sought out the mayor of Cajarc. The mayor is also the town druggist, and his establishment seems to be a club of sorts, like one of those storefront Mafia hangouts in Little Italy. There's always a group of local men sitting around, reading papers, watching soccer, whatever. You get the feeling that *everything* is discussed there.

When I arrived at the *pharmacie,* the mayor and the boys jumped up to greet me and said, all at once, Have a coffee, have a drink, sit down, welcome, monsieur. I told them about the problem and that I had written a letter to M. Carnac and I hoped that the mayor would give it to him. Well, this request caused five minutes of hilarity among the group. Finally, the mayor — when he could contain himself — told me that this act would be futile. M. Carnac can't read. He can file a lawsuit well enough, but never mind reading.

Just at this moment, M. Carnac himself came walking by the drugstore in the road. We all grew hushed as he moved past, his head down, pretending not to be aware of us. He wears a typical workingman's outfit of French blues (with very baggy knees) and sandals, but beyond that he is the most amazing-looking human: His arms are extraordinarily long and sinewy, like ape arms, and his head looks like two heads crushed together. He appears eerily Cro-Magnon, thousands of years old. I don't mean this description as an insult, as in this part of the world — something I really love about it, as I've told you before — you can actually see references in faces which go that far back. As he walked past, he was muttering, quite loudly, but I couldn't figure out what he was saying. The boys, however, knew exactly what he was saying and began mimicking him — "*imbécile . . . imbécile . . . ,*" this was *imbécile,* that was *imbécile* — to the rhythmic tapping of their heels. Apparently *imbécile* is his favorite word. He has no use for reading and writing, considers it a waste of energy and no doubt *imbécile.* One of the boys then nudged me and pointed to the WWI memorial outside the building. It is a beautiful and actually very soulful piece of ironwork, and I always admire it as I pass by. I looked quizzical, and then he shrugged and said that M. Carnac had made it. So paradoxes are everywhere in these parts.

Your son,
Tim

280 West 73d Street, New York

Dear Tim,

Ooh, la, la, I am really enjoying your battle with M. Carnac. Keep the stories coming. He is a character right out of Balzac — and maybe you didn't get around to Balzac's novels in your Harvard lit classes, but now's the time. The wily peasant is a familiar character. If nothing else, the books will disabuse you of an entirely romantic view of that part of the world. One of the things that always amazed me during my time in France was the French ability to put up with an extraordinary amount of "roughness," or *dur*, in their lives. On the one hand, the French can produce delicious food and objects of extraordinary beauty; and on the other hand, they can live with amazing indifference to dirt, damp, discomfort, bad air, bad showers, and bad toilets. Perhaps it's the conditioning of wartime, something they know a lot about. They were forced to put up with great hardship, and so the discipline continues. And perhaps they realize that there are higher priorities. When I lived in Paris, I rented a room from a Mme. Claudel. I later found out that she was from an extremely well off family, yet every day she trudged to the fifth floor, huffing and puffing, carrying her string bag full of groceries, and every day she took a cold bath in the bathroom that I shared with her. It wouldn't have occurred to her to live any differently.

Much love, Mom

Mas La Viguerie

Dear Mom,

Your wily Balzac peasant is having his fun with me. I was summoned by petition to the district court to explain myself, and so yesterday I had to get up very early for the court date. I had arranged to have Marce drive me and then go on to her office, so she stayed the night, but in the morning when we went outside the tires on her car were deflated. The work of the wily peasant? Most likely, but I won't be able to prove it. Anyway, I then had to bicycle fast and furiously to Figeac, as my *deux-chevaux* was with the mechanic, for *yet another* rest cure. What an experience in the court! There were three judges on the panel hearing cases — all of them female and all under thirty! Not exactly my image of the French judicial system. There was a lot of fast talk, but my French is just not good enough yet to figure what was going on. M. Carnac didn't show up, so I have to reappear in a month. Another one of his sneaky maneuvers, I'm sure.

Paul the boatman says that M. Carnac is notorious in these parts for making *eau de vie* in illegal quantities. It seems that individual production of alcohol is strictly regulated by the government — to protect the liquor industry, naturally, says Paul — but Carnac has his own distilling system and produces as much as he wants, way above the legal limits. He gets away with this because the government inspectors are completely terrified of him. Local lore has it that he actually killed one of them. The death was quite a few years ago, and no one is surprised that he has never been convicted of a crime. Oh, boy.

To get a break from my war with "Monsieur Bête," my new name for him, last week Marcelline and I drove to Ste.-Lucie d'Olt to visit her parents. M. and Mme. Becaze live about two hundred miles from my place in what is listed in guidebooks as one of the most charming villages in France, but not exactly on the tourist trail. Our drive over was great. We had a lot of fun together, and the beauty of this place, the *ségala* (chestnut forests), the limestone *causses*, green rolling hills . . . what I love about the Lot Valley is the way it spreads itself out before you in great waves, so you can appreciate every turn in the road.

It was Sunday and we stopped for lunch at a rather dreary-looking hotel café in a dreary nondescript town, consisting of bleak gray stone houses dead on the main road that runs through it. Inside the café, it was noisy and smoky and full of dogs — no problem bringing your dog into a French restaurant, I've discovered — and I was worried about what we would get to eat. But the meal turned out to be one of the most amazing I've had since moving here: a delicious trout *meunière*, so fresh it must have been lifted from the stream into the frying pan, a *frisée* salad, no doubt pulled minutes before from the garden, with the most incredible *vinaigrette*, and a rich apricot tart. Do I now sound too supergourmet? I think the French fanaticism about food is rubbing off on me.

Marce was very nervous about my meeting the folks. The house the Becazes live in was once a grand *demeure* in the nineteenth century, that is, a very big house, but not exactly a château, that was bombed out during the war . . . although I'm not quite sure which war. They live now in about one tenth of the building. It seems at some point they just moved in, kind of like homesteaders in the West. No one else claimed it and, truth to tell, there were few other people around who would want it. The Lot Valley never really recovered from the Wars of Religion hundreds of years ago, and then of course came more war, phylloxera, and just a whole lot of misery. Unlike in the United States, there was no FEMA, no relief money, so the valley lay essentially fallow for over a hundred years.

When we walked into the Becaze house through the front door, there was this amazing chiaroscuro effect created by the outside light streaming across the floor, which turned out to be made of dirt. There are also no indoor toilets. This sounds primitive, but the house is immaculate and very comfortable nonetheless.

Marcelline's father proudly says he is a twentieth-generation farmer. The land he farms is actually owned by *le patron*, as they refer to him, who lives in a big house up in the hills. Whenever *le patron*'s name came up, they automatically pointed up to the hills, as if in salute.

Marcelline seemed very embarrassed by the lack of indoor toilets, but Christ, what do I care? I get the impression that the parents actually have quite a bit of money. They sent all their children to college and they own a number of properties in the village. I tried to tell her that she should be proud of her family, but she got angry and said that I don't understand France, that I am being a silly romantic.

I have a feeling Marce had a plan to show me off to her parents, and at times I did feel like a piece of meat, but they were very gracious to me. Every evening at six, her father would be sitting at the kitchen table drinking a *pastis* and he would offer me one. Mother would be at the stove silently stirring her pots. Father would toast me with his glass, knock it back, and pour another. Needless to say, there wasn't a great flow of conversation. When he did say something, it was in rapid *patois* and nearly impossible to understand. Then we would sit down to eat the evening meal, which always began with a soup. Potato and leek the first night, then squash, lettuce, bean. All so delicious. I teased Marce that she had never made any of these soups for me, and she got very flustered; I don't have time, she said, I'm not in the kitchen all day. Hey, Marce, I said, I'm kidding, and I could see out of the corner of my eye that Mme. Becaze was pleased by the compliment. During one dinner, Marce's father asked me how I made a living. I tried to explain that I'm a trained mathematician but that I'm now working as an artist. I think I really confused him. He just stared at me blankly. *"À chacun son métier,"* he finally said and shrugged.

I got the impression that there was a lot a family drama going on under the surface, of which I did not get the full drift because of the heavy Midi accent. There was a lot of whispering at times. Something about Marce's sister and her husband, something about her mother's illness. Her mother did look very tired a lot of the time.

And in a place where the sheep outnumber the people, a new body in town is put under a microscope, so all through the day neighbors just *happened* to pop by. What a difference from New York, where people's lives are all so separate, and arriving without forewarning would be rude. Every single visitor was offered a coffee, a drink, a sweet, so poor Maman, not feeling well at all, was entertaining the neighbors every day because of me.

All in all, I had an interesting time. I did a lot of sketching, and at night Marce and I found some nifty places to hide out. One night, with a full moon blazing, we slept out in the hayloft of the barn. Another night we took blankets to a shepherd's hut up the hill. When we straggled into the house in the mornings, Maman gave us a grumpy look but said nothing. Then she put down big bowls of café au lait and slices of bread thick with butter and jam (a ravishing, homemade blueberry). I had a sense that mother and daughter had had some tense conversations, but Marce didn't let me in on what was said.

Marce got very moody on the drive back home and hardly talked at all. When things are good between us, they are very good, but when things are bad, it's hard to know what to do. When we are alone together we are absolutely at our best, but when the outside world gets factored in, stresses seem to come popping out of nowhere. It always gets me thinking that the American sense of how to live life is so different from the French. The problem is, I intuit the differences but I can't quite pinpoint them.

Your son,
Tim

Mas La Viguerie

Dear Mom,

Well, after yet another hellish week dealing with my crazed neighbor, M. Bête, I was ready for a little respite and I got it.

Today I had an enchanting experience. I drove over to Villefranche in the morning to bring my drawings to Mathilde Raymonde at her gallery. Did I tell you about her? She is a very enterprising woman, originally from Paris, who has managed to set up a successful gallery. She claims she can sell my drawings for a very nice price, so we'll see. I worked hard on them — in between working hard on the house — and I'm pretty proud of them. Anyway, when I walked into the gallery there was a woman there who, as I would find out, is a painter and sculptor. She had this wonderful look, what I would describe as bohemian-bourgeois, incredibly proud bearing, sandals, peasant skirt, hair pulled in a low bun, and lovely antique jewelry. Mathilde was in the other room dealing with a customer and so Mme. LeDuc and I ended up talking to each other. She let me look through her photo album of works. They were not exactly my cup of tea, as she does frankly religious stuff, very pure-looking, with zero edge, if you get my drift, but they were well executed. When I showed her my drawings — very sheepishly — she admired them with great gushes of enthusiasm and then made some serious and good suggestions. It turns out that she is on vacation in the Midi, where she comes every year with her husband and children for at least two months to stay at her family house. Apparently, her sister — who also paints, she says — lives there year-round, and she gave me her sister's name and phone number and then took mine. She was vehement that I had to meet her sister. "You'll love each other," she said.

After Mme. LeDuc left, Mathilde was very amused by the encounter. Well, she said, you certainly made a conquest there. Mme. is a Benoir (LeDuc being her married name), and they are very "old family" and a big deal in these parts. Their family spread is the Château de la Rive outside Cajarc. Not too shabby!

Your son,
Tim

Pauline LeDuc to her sister
Catherine Benoir

Chère Catherine,

I left so quickly without telling you any news, but we were in a hurry to get back to Paris. At Mathilde's gallery in the morning I met the most charming man. He is a young American, I'm not sure how old. You can never tell with Americans because they can look younger than they are, the way they dress! He has recently bought a property in St.-Jean d'Olt. He seems extremely intelligent and was showing Mathilde some of his drawings. He draws extremely well, and I mentioned you to him. I told him that you had taken up painting again and that you should get to know each other, as you will have a lot to talk about. I worry that in the winter you are so isolated, and here is someone who can provide some interesting conversation. I'm sure you will like him. You should think of inviting him to lunch next Sunday. Pierre and I will arrive some time on Friday.

I embrace you,
Pauline

Catherine Benoir to her sister Yvette Benoir,
Château de la Rive

Chère Yvette,

Pauline left again yesterday without discussing a thing

47

about Tante Marie's cottage. As soon as I bring up the subject, she always claims she has to rush off to Paris. We are desperate for money, and if we spent just a little on fixing the cottage up, it could bring in significant income, but she won't come to grips with the problem. She keeps talking of retaining the "spirit of our château." Strangers living in the cottage, she claims, would spoil her memories of our early family life. This is silly and completely impractical. But you know how she is. It is impossible to reason with her. And because we must all agree, we will never agree. Oh, how could our father have put us in such a position — although maybe we should blame Napoleon and his wretched laws. I had to walk for hours to calm myself down.

In the same note to me, Pauline asked me to invite to lunch a young American man she met in Mathilde's gallery. You know Pauline, probably flirting again, playing the grande dame, then claiming she feels sorry for me stuck away in the country with no one to talk to and so she has to help her *pauvre soeur*. When I lived alone in Paris, no one in the family thought I needed any special care. I was a sophisticated Parisian woman with her own life, but now that I live here I am *pauvre soeur*, just another unmarried woman. Pauline has also recently anointed me "the sainted one" because I took care of Maman in her last years: Catherine is our heroine, how she sacrificed for the family, how we look up to her, and on and on. You might wonder why this bothers me so, as it seems at first a compliment. In fact, it makes me feel controlled and confined to the "sainted" role. It implies that I am so pure and holy that I have no choice but to retire, as if to a convent, to spend my last days doing good works.

How can people in families be so different — some so opaque, others so deeply feeling and empathetic? Remember what Maman used to say about us? You were water, always flowing in and out silently. I was air, always whooshing around or floating away. Pauline was earth, moving heavily and slowly on the ground, and popping out all those children! Pauline was always so different, even from Maman, who could observe what was going on around her with such humor and detachment. Today especially I missed her terribly.

I embrace you,
Catherine

Mas La Viguerie

Dear Mom,

To my amazement, Mlle. Benoir, Mme. LeDuc's sister, called during the week to invite me to lunch, and today I went to Château de la Rive, a day without a cloud in the sky and the air like silk. I don't know what I was expecting, but it was so much more extraordinary than anything I could have imagined.

The entrance to the château is actually no big deal. In

fact, I passed right by it on the road, as I guess I had conjured up Versailles-like grandeur, a great long drive or some such thing, and so had to backtrack. You enter the property right smack off the road and into a circular driveway. What you see at first is essentially a three-story blond-stone manor house, very, very nice, very architecturally pleasing, but not overwhelming if you're looking for a château.

Mme. LeDuc — "call me Pauline" — came to the door to greet me. She then led me through a large cluttered rectangular foyer — with paintings hung floor to ceiling — which cut through the center of the house to a set of double doors that opened onto the back. As we walked outside, I had to catch my breath, literally, as I suddenly saw where I *really* was, in a magnificent *parc* that seemed to extend for acres and acres, with terraced gardens, an *orangerie*, tennis court, numerous vegetable gardens, rose gardens, and vineyards cascading down to the river. I could hardly take it all in.

Under a giant cedar tree, a few women were setting four large rectangular tables for lunch. (Later I realized they were daughters-in-law, shades of your daughter-in-law story!) Mme. LeDuc, who held me tightly by the arm, said that we would be having lunch in a half-hour and then introduced me to a young blond woman named Valerie. She suggested that Valerie show me the grounds. Valerie blushed several shades of red, and I got the impression that Mme. LeDuc was pushing us together, but

I could have been mistaken. Maybe Valerie is just a very shy girl.

Anyway, Valerie walked me through the *parc* to see the vineyards, which terrace down to the river. She explained that the property had ten hectares of vineland, and that the château produces a small number of bottles every year under its own label. It used to be a much bigger operation, but they have scaled back, and this year the wine has been very good. She said that she was studying viniculture and then said a lot of other things about the type of grapes grown, but this whole wine-growing thing is still an unknown subject for me and I just nodded along. I tried to make a little joke about how little I knew, and she looked at me really strangely. I have no idea what she thought I said, and I hope it wasn't too awful.

As we walked back toward the house, sunlight was bouncing off the immense cedar tree, the tables had red and white tablecloths, the place settings were a wild variety of the brightest blues and yellows, and about a dozen small blond children were scooting around on little tricycles. I kept thinking, Is this place for real? Are these people for real? Have I time-traveled back to a scene in a Renoir painting?

Forty people sat down to lunch, as casual as can be. As I would discover, most of them were Pauline's offspring, their wives and/or husbands, and the assorted grandchildren. The little children were amazingly polite and full of fun — not wild and loud and out of control as American kids would be. There must have been at least twenty multicolored tricycles scattered around the lawn. The kids all seem to have double names for some reason, like Lisette-Marie, Paul-Henri. It was hard to keep track. Pauline LeDuc and her husband, Pierre — a tall, big-boned man with wild hair and a shambling walk — are at the château for their annual sojourn. All their children with their various offspring are there as well. They stay mainly in what I guess is the "adjunct château." I don't know what it was originally. Maybe where the staff lived at the turn of the century? Anyway, now there is no staff at all that I could see, except for two local women who helped bring out food from the kitchen.

The lunch was very simple and almost all of it had been produced in the château gardens: several different kinds of omelets, tomatoes, zucchini, green bean salad, melons, peaches, figs. As we ate the food, we also talked about it. Weren't the figs delicious? . Figs are my absolute favorite . . . The peach trees ripened late this year . . . The melons are not as good as last year. I went into sensual food overload, just soaking it all in, letting it wash over me.

I was seated at a table next to Mme. LeDuc's sister Catherine Benoir. Sitting on the other side of her was one of her young grandnieces, and they were sweet with each other, laughing together over their little private jokes.

Mlle. Benoir was very charming to me. She had a lot of questions about my house and its origins. She said she had never been to my commune, and I invited her to visit when she had time. I told her that I had recently discovered that the round brick structure on my property is a *pigeonnier* and that I was fascinated by it. Since my previous experience of pigeons consisted of watching Marlon Brando in *On the Waterfront* tend them on his rooftop — not to mention the piles of bird poop all over New York — I said I was interested to see that pigeon keeping was a hobby in France, too. Oh no, not a hobby, she told me. Over centuries, on the farmlands of France, pigeon manure was highly prized given that other kinds of manure were so much harder to obtain. A *pigeonnier* on the property was a sign of wealth. When she saw my reaction, she laughed, recognizing right away that I wasn't exactly Farmer Tim yet.

And so the day just drifted by. If it were not the French countryside, it could have been a lazy day in Chekhov's Russia. Think *The Seagull*. The more I live here, the more I realize that in France "eating" is not just shoveling some stuff down your throat, but a semireligious rite, as it gives the double opportunity of good food and good talk, two forms of aesthetic enjoyment the French really value. I can understand how over time the appreciation of food became an antidote to chaos. During the endless religious wars, even if there was little to eat, life continued in its intrinsically French way. Your neighbor might be accused of heresy, but one sat down with a good piece of bread, *foie gras,* and a bottle of wine no matter what.

At some point, I began a very quick sketch of one of the children on a paper napkin. She was so excited by it that her enthusiasm spread like a virus to all the *minuscules* — Catherine Benoir's name for the littlest children — and created quite a commotion. So then I had to make yet another little sketch, then another, until finally the mothers reined in the children, and I promised I would come back to make more sketches. I got a lot of compliments from the adults: how quickly I drew, so accurate, so beautiful, *merveilleux, splendide.*

The sisters told many stories of their childhood and their parents. I have come to admire the French spirit and toughness. I have also come to understand completely their hostility to the invasion of American fast food and Franglais. They have over two thousand years of continuous history, and here comes this flashy new stuff from the outside, with nothing especially positive to offer, just perhaps, oh, the complete destruction of their society. Change may be inevitable, but for the French, tradition is an anchor. Change without underpinning, without good soil beneath it, is just scorched earth. It seems to me that their fierceness in protecting their identity and traditions is what has kept this land together for so long.

By the end of the afternoon, I was both tired and flying high, as if I had been smoking dope all afternoon.

Your son,
Tim

Mas La Viguerie

Dear Mom,

Mlle. Benoir stopped by today with her nephew Roger. He helps her with a lot of the gardening at the château. They brought some cuttings with them from a gorgeous climbing rose that I admired when I was there for lunch. She swept out past the house into the garden, then immediately sank down into the only outdoor chair, a horrible rickety piece of junk, but it fortunately didn't collapse on impact. She seemed oblivious to any discomfort and looked perfectly at ease as she surveyed the landscape. She exclaimed about this tree and that tree, *exquis, superbe.* It seems that the ex–city boy didn't really know what he had. I ran into the house and got a notepad and then I asked her to walk around with me. She smiled at the notepad but she consented, and then as we walked she identified every single tree for me. I seriously wanted to put Post-its on all the trees but then I thought, Better restrain myself. So with Mlle. Benoir's help, I have managed to identify all the trees on my property. Walnut and cherry, you'll be happy to know, make up the bulk of them. I can't exactly explain why, but this knowledge gave me an almost otherworldly sense of peace, and I actually feel that the land is in some way more my own now.

Mlle. Benoir affects a kind of sophisticated peasant look, a shirred blouse, straw hat, long skirt. I'm not sure how old she is, but despite her age she has that French-woman's way of always being very gay and bubbly and light, and at the same time doling out little bits of criticism. I told her this and she laughed and laughed, and said, How true.

I asked her advice about my dispute with M. Bête. The latest is that he has gone to court yet again, claiming that not only did I block passage of his flock, but I also caused the death of his favorite ewe. Being a very sensitive soul, the ewe missed the stroll through my land and died of homesickness. I'm not joking. Mlle. Benoir listened very carefully, then smiled slyly. I have a suggestion, she said, but perhaps you won't like it. I insisted I could take whatever was coming. Okay, she said, what if you just took the stones down and let the sheep through? Then she laughed at my reaction. You have to understand these people, she said. What is M. Carnac really fighting about? He's taking nothing from you personally, he just wants to continue his way of life. I was at first very resistant to her idea. I am so furious at what he's put me through. But then I realized she was right. My instinct was, Hey, the world moves on, just screw him, but apparently that ends up screwing me,

She told me that her family has been involved in many land disputes. In fact, they have been locked in a property dispute going back two hundred years with a neighboring château belonging to the Comte de Poisson, and it is still in the courts! She said the Comte de Poisson (oh yes, he is the "Count of Fish") claims lineage from Mme. de Pompadour, whose family name was also Poisson. "The only true aristocrat from far and wide," she says he calls himself; no one else measures up. She said she had very little use for *particules*. Most of the "de"s are phonies, she says. She promised to take me to Poisson's château. I asked if they were on speaking terms, given that they were involved in a lawsuit, and she laughed loudly: Of course! But, she added, Poisson, in fact, always does all the talking. She said that Poisson would know everything about my house, which really intrigued me. Mlle. Benoir has a detached/engaged quality. Very mysterious. I'm not sure what I think about it. Sometimes I think I am being played with — *moqué,* as the French would say.

Catherine — she insisted I call her that — and Roger actually ended up staying for dinner. I was very nervous about it, as you know how much "entertaining" I have done before — zero. I was absolutely positive I had nothing for them to eat, but Catherine somehow managed to find enough with salad, cheese, some ham, bread, and, thank God, I had a bottle of wine.

I learned a lot about the family's Catholicism. I dropped into the conversation that I was reading Pascal — not to impress or anything, of course not. Anyway, Catherine asked if I knew that Pascal was a Jansenist, which I didn't, and she said her great-grandfather had been one. Jansen was a Dutchman who practiced a very strict Catholicism — as if it wasn't strict enough back then — and Great-Granddaddy was one of them. Similar to Calvinism, she said. I took French history, but I didn't pay much attention to the religious tugs of war. At the time they seemed bizarre to me, just inexplicable fighting over arcane differences between this sect and that sect. I can't see how Jansenism applies to the Benoirs, except perhaps that everything is *vulgaire* and *affreux*, and they have a very strict moral code. But they laugh a lot and are a lot of fun for people so strict.

Catherine's sister Pauline is apparently fanatically religious and pals around with a lot of bishops and cardinals. Roger, who is Pauline's son, had lots to say about this and at one point got so agitated that Catherine had to calm him down. Roger seems to be rebelling against his mother's domination, he's the only son who isn't married, and, boy, does he hear about it. After they left, I tried to read some more Pascal. Sometimes it's heavy going, but I'm working up to reading his famous proof of God's existence. Thinking about God was something people of his time did every day, right up there with having breakfast, lunch, and dinner.

Your son,
Tim

Château de la Rive

Chère Yvette,

Yesterday I went with Roger to the farm of the young American, Tim Reinhart. He is very enthusiastic about his new farm and full of energy, so we had quite a lively time. I brought him cuttings from our rosebushes, which he had admired when he came for lunch. Then he asked me to walk around the property with him to identify his trees, making it obvious that he is very much *un homme de la ville* — a city boy, as he called himself. When I got home, I was stirred to think about how different our life is from an American one. Imagine if you or I just picked up and moved to the United States, just bought a property and began fixing it up. Unthinkable. Tim has that American directness, not layered over by centuries of manners, and that American optimism. Maybe that's why I like American comedies so much, instead of our own comedies with their melancholy and anomie. Perhaps my liking certain American things goes back to the Americans saving France when I was a child. In any case . . .

Please let me know when you think I should come up to Paris to help you with the accountants . . . but, oh my God, how I dread talking to those people.

I embrace you,
Catherine

Mas La Viguerie

Dear Mom and Dad,

Yesterday Catherine Benoir took Marcelline and me to visit the Comte de Poisson. This trip would have been right up your alley, Mom, drop-dead novel material. Marce — in her up-and-down way — was alternately eager and reluctant to go, but I couldn't imagine passing on an opportunity to see this place, so we went.

The Poisson château dates back to the fifteenth century and is older, but smaller, than the Benoir château, which is more beautiful and has a lot more land. The two places are within a mile of each other.

Le Comte de Poisson claims the more illustrious lineage. According to him, the Benoir family is *haute bourgeoisie* — not really royal, just a few noble streams — whereas the Poisson lineage is super-royal. Catherine brushed him off laughingly. She claims to be grateful for not being encumbered with her family's pedigree. Takes your energy, she says, keeps you from moving forward. But the Benoirs were much, much richer at the turn of the century and Fishy's château has seen better times. He is the first royalist I've ever met. He sincerely wants the monarchy to be restored.

As Fishy made his case for the return of the monarchy, Catherine kept rolling her eyes. Marce, who looked uncomfortable from the moment we arrived, left to walk the grounds. I, of course, was riveted by his wacko sincerity. The eighteenth century is like yesterday to him.

But now he lives in just two derelict downstairs rooms. We sat in enormous dusty red armchairs — very Louis Something — in front of a gigantic fireplace that you could step into. The only lighting was a bare bulb hanging precariously from a once gorgeous but now completely dirt-encrusted chandelier. To serve us, Fishy pushed away the papers that he was working on from his enormous all-purpose blackened pine table. Our feast consisted of coffee with lots of milk and stale cake. Catherine told me later that Fishy has absolutely no money, except for what he can make from the château antiques he sells off. She also said that there is a wife but that no one has seen her for years.

After going on and on about his lineage, Fishy suddenly dropped the astounding news that my farm was used by the Maquis, the French resistance fighters during WWII. They actually lived in my house for over nine months! Fishy says there is a passage somewhere that runs underground, then opens onto a field near a roadside *crèche*. Fishy was sure he could find it and offered to come over and search it out with me. He claimed that his first wife was an informer and had "outed" her own father. When I looked astonished, he just shook his head and said that father and daughter never did get along! In this part of the world, resentment toward collaborators still runs very high. I asked him about the memorial to partisans at the bridge near my *mas,* and he promised he would go there with me and describe the night the bridge was blown up.

As we were heading home, I was all fired up by what I had just learned. Marcelline got grumpy. She said it was old, ridiculous stuff, the man was a complete idiot, and why was I even interested in him. We got into quite a bang-up fight. I said, Yeah, maybe he was a nasty old asshole, but so what, I was interested in what he had to say, I was interested in the experience of the place, etc., etc. By the time we got home, Marce had calmed down and became very sweet and apologetic. She has the ability to change her mood on a dime. I can't do that. I had to wait until the morning before I could act as if nothing happened.

The owner of Marcelline's place has let her know that she has to move, as he wants to rent it to his wife's relatives. This news puts an unspoken pressure on us, as she will need to move pretty soon. She spends almost all of her time here now, and she has been great about helping me make the place more livable, and so of course there is the possibility of MOVING IN TOGETHER. We get along great in the youknowwhat department, but needless to say living together is another deal completely.

Tim

Mas La Viguerie

Dear Mom,

This morning I rode my bike into Villefranche to see Mathilde, the gallery owner. The fact that the *deux-cheveaux* keeps breaking down means I have to use my bike a lot, and if nothing else my conditioning is improving.

I got an early start and by eight A.M. I was up a very steep road, heading south. It had rained the night before and was a bit overcast when I started out, but then the sun burned through and mist began rising off the pavement. A knockout gorgeous morning. I love riding my bike on this road. You follow the Lot along the top of the *causse* so it's a steep ride up but then smooth sailing along the flat top of the plateau. The Lot is the snakiest river I've ever seen — if you pulled it straight, it would be twice as long — it just twists and twists and twists, and only about fifty miles is actually navigable. On one stretch, I got caught behind a truck full of pigs creating an unbelievable stink.

Mathilde has managed to sell a series of my drawings of the Causse de Limogne dolmens, for not a *whole* lot of money, but it's my first sale. She teased me about Pauline LeDuc. Apparently every time Pauline comes into the gallery, she talks about me. *What a charming man! How delightful his drawings are!* Mathilde thinks Pauline, who is very tenacious, is looking to fix me up with Valerie, the blond woman I met at lunch at the château. I appreciate her interest in finding female companionship for me, but I would prefer to do my own choosing!

Mathilde and I had lunch at a café around the corner from the gallery. Between the *steak-frites* and the *tarte Tatin*, I got a real earful about the Benoirs. She said that an older brother, Louis, died very recently. Apparently, he was a big deal in Paris, very *haut* in the government, she says, and Catherine was close to him. After he died, he left Catherine and Yvette without a ballast against sister Pauline's powerful juggernaut. Pauline has nine children and they are all, except one (Roger), married. That makes three son-in-laws and five daughter-in-laws, and they all show up at the château in the summer with their respective broods. The other sister, Yvette, lives in Paris, has no children, and is very artistic and lovely but retiring.

According to Mathilde, their mother was a great beauty in her day and an accomplished pianist. In the 1980s, she became ill and moved from Paris to live full-time in the château. At some point, Catherine moved down to take care of her, and after her mother died, Catherine decided to remain at the château. I asked Mathilde why Catherine had never married. She hesitated, as if worrying about being indiscreet, but then said that she was told there had been a very long relationship with a man, someone quite prominent, but that she thinks it ended when Catherine decided to live in the Midi permanently.

Your son,
Tim

Mas La Viguerie

Dear Mom,

This morning Marcelline and I got into *yet another* conversation about moving in together.

One of the pressing factors is that she has to move very soon, and there is really nowhere else for her to rent nearby, which means she will have to live in Villefranche or else try to get a job in Toulouse, which would mean we could see each other only on weekends. So of course the most *convenient* thing is for her to move in here. I really do understand her dilemma, and I know I am not making it easy for her. From what I can sense, Marcelline lives in a constant state of anxiety . . . what will happen to me? . . . will I marry? . . . will I have children? To be honest, I'm not sure that our respective anxieties mesh, and I'm not sure I am getting a full story from her.

In the middle of our discussion, I suddenly remembered that I was expected at Catherine's for lunch. I told Marce that she was welcome to come with me, but she shook her head fiercely and made all sorts of faces. She has all these very mobile expressions, which are wonderful to draw, but not always so wonderful to experience.

When I got to Catherine's, she was there by herself and getting ready to leave for Paris tomorrow. She was worried about all the workmen at the house, who are shoring up a piece of roof that completely collapsed a few nights ago. So I offered to housesit sort of, that is, turn up during the day when the workmen are about.

After lunch, we brought coffee outside onto the terrace and sat looking out at the gardens. (Drinking coffee outside after a meal is one of the Benoirs' rituals, and a pretty nice one.) Catherine seemed in a particularly thoughtful mood, and I heard for the first time the story of what happened to her family in the war. As soon as I got home, I started this letter so that it would be fresh in my mind. You have been nudging me to get the dope, so here it is.

Catherine's family was living in Paris, and her mother was pregnant with her when the Germans entered the city in June 1940. The entire French government immediately fled Paris and so did the Benoirs, along with a mass exodus of Parisians. The Benoir cars had been requisitioned by the French government for the war effort, so the family piled into an ancient borrowed van, along with the gas and provisions they had been hoarding in anticipation of the German occupation. Only one servant came with them.

There was no radio communication or mail for several months. There was also little fuel, and the family both cooked and boiled their laundry in vats in the great stone fireplace in the main room. Catherine was born at the château in September 1940 and can thereby say she is a genuine Cajarcoise.

Apparently, the château — which originally dates back

to the sixteenth century — was rebuilt by Catherine's paternal great-grandfather in the 1860s. It had been almost totally destroyed during the Wars of Religion. The great-grandfather became very rich in Paris; it was a time of prosperity, and he was determined to restore the family château. Even when phylloxera hit the vineyards in the 1870s, his wealth was protected, as winemaking was not his main source of income. The family remained a power in the region, and Catherine's father was revered locally during WWII, as he secretly funded many Resistance missions.

In 1944 the war was at a critical point and the Germans requisitioned the château. The Benoirs — with three-year-old Catherine, her older brother, Louis, and Pauline (Yvette had not yet been born) — went back to Paris. Their apartment in Paris had also been requisitioned (Jesus Christ!), so they had to find a hotel to live in. The whole lot of them lived in two small rooms until the war was finally over and they could go back to their apartment in the rue de Varenne. But the parents were permanently scarred, and their life in Paris took on a more somber tone. The war had exhausted them, and Catherine remembers thinking of them as very old.

To be continued. She promises that the next chapter will cover her youth in Paris. I can't wait to hear what she did in the swinging sixties!

Tim

Château de la Rive

Dear Holly,

After three days in Milan, and two in Paris, we arrived late last night for our visit with your brother. We are not staying as originally planned at the hotel in Cajarc, as his friend Catherine Benoir insisted on putting us up at her château — and I being a fool for a château agreed to this! So Tim picked us up at the train station and drove us directly there.

I had no idea what we would be in for. Now, out of politeness, we are stuck here, as it would be too rude to move. First of all, much of the château is abandoned to deteriorate at its own pace. You can almost hear crumbling bits falling to the ground in the night as you sleep. In fairness, it is clear that at one time there were masses of servants to attend to every need, but now there is little money for that. Salons full of exquisite eighteenth-century furniture are covered in dust sheets, piles of chipped Sèvres china and faience are everywhere left to their own devices. Old and rare books are left to curdle, valuable paintings, impressionist, Oriental, eighteenth-century, etc., with damaged frames and water stains, are hung this way and that everywhere, abandoned to eventually disintegrate.

To an American eye it is shocking, but Tim says the Benoirs are land-rich, and there is little money left for actual living. Every cent goes toward keeping up the properties, and they are forced to live very frugally. Fuel is very expensive, and fixing the most important things like leaks in the roof always comes first. He also says that to do anything in the château, all three sisters must agree, and because they never agree, nothing gets done. And nothing can be sold. Sounds hellishly frustrating.

The most important functions of life are taken care of by a *femme de ménage* who comes in twice a week, so the kitchen is kept clean, linens are washed, beds are changed, but comfort is another matter. No attention is paid to it, and no money put to it. They simply shut their eyes to what they can do nothing about. Our bathroom is actually on the floor above our bedroom and has all the amenities, but it's hardly convenient. Poor Dad ends up stumbling up the stairs in the middle of the night.

If not thrilled with the bathroom situation, your dad is completely fascinated by the stables. They are unused now, as the family no longer keep horses, but obviously at the turn of the century the stables were an important part of life at the château. Dad found an old touring car in one of the rooms, a Delaunay-Belleville, he says, a remnant of the Benoirs' once luxurious way of life. He said it looked as if it had been driven for the last time over fifty years ago and has been gathering dust ever since. He is obsessed with this car and says it was a favorite of the tsar of Russia.

He also says that generations of a family can follow a pattern of what he calls "Buildup, Eatup, Degeneration." The first generation is Buildup; they are in the vanguard, they make the wealth and have all the newest things. Then the second generation is Eatup; they spend the wealth and live large; and the third generation is Degeneration; the wealth is gone and life is now lived in the rear guard. And I must say, this theory fits the Benoirs.

I am fascinated by Mlle. Benoir's life here. Much of her day is spent trying to restore the château gardens. You can't believe how much land they have. She took me for a tour and described what she is planning. She does much of the work herself, with the help of one gardener and her nephew Roger when he's there, and they are now restoring a large pond with a curved bridge crossing over it. Very charming.

Last night, after dinner, we were treated to a photographic tour of family life at the turn of the century. They have this extraordinary old machine called a veriscope that slowly cranks out pictures. The pictures go back to the beginning of the century, and it was fascinating to see the progression in clothes and attitude. The third sister, Yvette, was here visiting, and she and Mlle. Benoir narrated. It was so lively and funny. The two sisters have pet names for each other, which is apparently very common in France among the upper classes. Catherine is Catsu, and the sister is Googoo. They explained how these names came about, and though my French is pretty good I couldn't quite grasp the anecdotes, as they kept interrupting each other with gales of laughter. Yvette is very lovely and sweet-tempered and moves in and out of rooms like a cat. Catherine says she is a very accomplished singer and in Paris devotes herself to arranging recitals throughout the year. When at the château, she spends most of her days listening to Maria Callas records in her room and watching reruns on TV of *Columbo*. Apparently, she never misses a *Columbo*!

Based on the photos, Catherine was quite the dish when she was young. There are many photos of her playing tennis with the other siblings on their court. Mlle. played tennis competitively — for a time she lived in London and played in tournaments there. She still has a lithe body and youthful walk. In later photographs — I'm guessing from the seventies and eighties — Catherine is shown with a mysterious-looking man. He keeps appearing, as if from behind a tree. I leaned over to Yvette at one point and asked his name. She became very serious . . . *Un philosophe, très important.* She told me his name, but I couldn't quite catch it. He looked very dashing, in that gaunt and moody French *philosophe* way.

I am so glad that Tim has discovered Mlle. Benoir. She is so charming and still lovely, considering she is pushing sixty. I asked Tim if there was a man in her life, and he laughed and said, Look at what she has to choose from in this town! Besides, she is a devout Catholic and marriage is a very sacred thing to her. He was so solemn, I didn't recognize my own son.

Yesterday we met his girlfriend, Marcelline — who is certainly very attractive in a dark, intense way — but it was somewhat tricky to communicate with her. When she answers your questions, she turns her head away. I can't attribute the difficulty completely to a language problem, as her English is very serviceable and my French is still good enough. Tim says she is so, so shy, but then suddenly she is full of energy and trying to explain everything about France to us as if she were our guide. She is clearly very intelligent and tries hard to please. So we'll see. Time will tell.

One morning I peeked into Mlle. Benoir's bedroom. It is for me the most delicious room in the house. Almost square, with tall windows looking out onto the *parc* and exquisite creamy wallpaper in a pattern of what looked like hummingbirds woven through blue helical ribbon stripes. The bed had a teester in the shape of a royal crown, with a gauzy fabric hanging down. Ravishing. Later I got up my courage to ask Catherine about the room, and she said it had originally been her mother's. She first occupied it when her mother was ill and became necessary to move her to the ground floor. Yes, she said, it is a perfect room, and she complimented me on recognizing this. The architect who did the restoration of the house was very famous in his day, and the master suite of rooms that had originally been used by her great-grandparents, then grandparents, then her parents, was a model of superior design. From time to time, architecture students from all over the country ask to visit. I can believe it.

I have a feeling that there are many, many secrets in this house. One night in bed (as a luscious new moon shone through the window), I told your father that I thought the life here was so *triste* underneath. What a struggle these French people have had! Living through two world wars, one right after the other, only twenty-two years in between. Second acts are not as easy in France as they are in America. Tradition binds the French and they don't have the American flexibility of just reinventing themselves and going on to an entirely new life.

My first reaction to your brother's farm was dead shock. It was both better and worse than I expected. Better because the land is so pure and beautiful, taking me back to family summers in the Berkshires, living with sweet, pure air and majestic trees — the respite we sought after a winter in the city. But the farmhouse itself, though picturesque, is ultimately very primitive. Tim still has miles to go before it is really comfortable.

Your brother has changed so much. It is so odd, seeing him outside a known framework. He looks so different now. Not "bad" different, just "different" different. The mother thing, I suppose: on the one hand this transformation breaks my heart and on the other it makes it soar.

It's hard to know what to think about it all. What he is doing now is so outside the parameters of our parental expectations. But I fight my own rigidities, and that is *always* good.

After several days of struggling with the *matelas* (mattress) on our bed, I hit the wall. I could barely move my neck and was in horrific pain. Notwithstanding its exquisite headboard, our bed is *au fond* just a two-hundred-year-old hammock full of lumps and dust. In desperation, I checked the local chamber of commerce and found a list of *kinésiologistes* (chiropractors to you). On the way to my appointment, I came upon the weekly market in the town square. Very picturesque and, despite my pain, I had to take a detour through it. And what do you think? In between the vendors for *viandes* and *poissons,* were two robust French girls selling mattresses! I went up to talk to them and they boxed me in on both sides, immediately selling me hard. I began amortizing in my head the future cost of chiropractors and perhaps weeks of pain, inability to write, etc. And then out of the corner of my eye I got a glimpse of a statue of the Virgin Mary in front of a little rectory. I swear that the Virgin was smiling at me and egging me on. So I thanked her profusely and then paid a fortune for the cheapest mattress they had. Later that afternoon the robust French girls — real toughies, they seemed delirious to be in a château and kept asking me if anything was for sale — hauled the mattress up to our bedroom. I'm sure the Benoirs, Catherine and Yvette, were horrified at the behavior of this crazy American woman, but at least I will sleep well at night, without pain, until we leave.

We will be back in New York on the 18th. Dad sends his love and so do I,

Mom

Mas La Viguerie

Dear Sis,

Being preggers is absolutely no excuse to turn down an invitation for a week in glorious southwest France. Seriously, you were very missed, and you missed an incredible time. Mom was Mom, Dad was Dad, but on the whole the parents behaved quite well, and it was fun to view them out of their element and working so hard on their politeness and sophistication. We did a lot of local touring, and Mom was able to practice her French and show off how much she knows about everything, and even I didn't realize how much she knows about French literature. She and Catherine really seemed to get along, so I'm happy about that.

Did she tell you about the whole *matelas* brouhaha? How she just went out in the morning, bought a new mattress, and had it delivered to the château! It was that side of Mom that has to get something done now. It was *so* not French. Fortunately, Catherine found it amusing.

She laughed and laughed and said she has been trying to get the mattresses changed for years, but that her sister Pauline won't hear of it. Pauline claims to prefer the old mattresses, because the grandchildren like to jump on them. Can you believe this?

After you finally pop, I'm expecting you, Brad, and baby to make an appearance asap.

Bro

Park Slope, Brooklyn

Dear Bro,

I haven't moved from the club chair by our bay window for what seems like days and days. My belly is the size of a gigantic watermelon, but I still have weeks to go. Oh, big brother, I am really missing you now. Getting your letter cracked my heart open. Isn't life the strangest, weirdest thing? How has it come to this? For so many years we spent every single day together just about, and now we don't exist in each other's space at all . . . not out of lack of feeling, not out of lack of interest, but out of where life has taken us.

I have been so wrapped up in this pregnancy. I never thought I'd be one of those women completely consumed with every little body change, but I am. And let's not get into the complex struggles with Spouse Brad. Things have calmed down because now I'm so big that I don't care about working, but for the first months I still had tons of energy, and as you know Brad turned out to be an extremely nervous expectant father. I have *his* child inside me and I am supposed to obey his every command. This behavior is not at all what I expected from him. In fact, I had nightmares when I first got pregnant that he would lose interest in me and start screwing around. Please remember the following very important information: marriage changes everything. Before marriage: a person you think you know and love. After marriage: a completely different person. When baby-making commences: a different country altogether!

Anyway, once the baby does arrive and things settle down somewhat, I promise to be better at writing. I must say, you certainly seem to have quite an exciting social life, considering that Mom was sure you would turn into a grungy old hermit over there. Being adopted by the rich château people is not exactly a bad deal, bro. And then he has a gorgeous French girlfriend as well! Please send me more news of French girlfriend. Mom read to me from your letters, but you can't have told her everything!

Love, Holly

Mas La Viguerie

Dear Sis,

I really miss you, too. True, we didn't get to see each other as much in the city after you hooked up with Brad, but we still had the occasional late-night pizza on Broadway. Now I've gone and spoiled it all by moving here. I think Americans in general have become more and more migratory, making it difficult for siblings to stay close and keep in touch. But here in France, family members can't get away from one another! Take the Benoir family: because their finances and housing are completely commingled, they can't disentangle themselves and they stay stuck in the web, until they go out feet-first. Which is worse, I don't know.

How to tell you more about Marcelline? You're catching me at a time when things are not going so well between us. When she is sweet, she is very, very sweet, but when she has a bee in her bonnet, Christ! After we got back from a visit with her family awhile back, Marce was moody for days. I couldn't figure it out. She gets a lot of stress from her family, I think. She can remind me of you a little in the way she throws herself into a new enthusiasm. She becomes giddy with excitement, and right now she's learning to play the piano. One of my big difficulties with her is defensiveness. When we go to a museum together, she hates the idea that she doesn't know something. She would rather pretend, and this drives me crazy. Another problem is that when I take her to see my friend Catherine Benoir, she gets all bent out of shape. She is actually jealous of my friendship with Catherine. I don't want to give up this friendship, as it has become important to me.

I've been going over to the Benoir château a couple of afternoons a week. There is a painting studio there that Catherine's mother once used, and it has the most wonderful atmosphere and perfect light. Catherine has told me that I can use it whenever I like. Sometimes late in the afternoon, when I have worked there, and our respective painting times are over, we sit out in the garden and talk about what we have done in the day. It is just technical stuff, but I get a lot from it. We don't always agree — in fact we frequently disagree — but no matter what, it's great to be able to hash out problems. She is herself struggling to find a way to paint again. There was a period in Paris when she had a modest success, as she calls it, but for nearly ten years — after she came to live in the Midi — she didn't paint at all, and now she is pushing herself to find her way back. Her work is really quite good, very impressionistic, very Mary Cassatt, and I'm encouraging her to take more chances. Talk about painting is our template, and from there we can go anywhere we want in the universe. We just fly along without a stop. So many times I look at my watch and realize that we have been talking for hours, and it had seemed like minutes.

She is also working on a biography of Mme. de Maintenon, the last wife of Louis XIV. She became interested in her while a student at the Sorbonne. She claims that Mme. de Maintenon was much maligned by the savage writings of the French courtiers, particularly someone named Saint-Simon, I think that's his name.

Looming over Marcelline and me is the issue of moving in together. Marce is very earthbound, which in many ways I like very much. It translates into a lovely naturalness about living, and for a city boy it has been a revelation, but she is not big on abstractions. For her, this is this, that is that. Stepping back and looking at the larger picture is not for her. Sometimes I get the weird feeling that for Marcelline I am just a body — just as Pauline Le-Duc's husband was the body that gave her nine children. I can really feel that atavistic pull in Marcelline to live this prescribed French life.

When I came to live here, I thought I would be dealing with just my work and my property, but I am completely locked in uncertainty and anxiety about my relationship with Marcelline. Fortunately, Brian is coming soon and we are going on a bike trip. It will get me out of here for a couple of weeks!

Your Bro

Catherine Benoir,
Rue de Varenne, Paris

Dear Tim,

Thank you so much for dealing with the carpenters and with M. Ver showing up at the château. He was a close friend of my father, and in his will my father left him all the old harnesses in the stables. So now he has finally come to pick them up, after twenty years! I really wonder what he wants with them now.

Old M. Ver showing up makes me think back to when our family drove down to the château after the war. I think I was ten, so it must have been 1950, and we had not been in the Midi since leaving in such a hurry in 1944 when the Germans commandeered the property.

On the drive down, I remember being very excited. I had fixed in my mind the beautiful photographs of the château. Almost every night, according to my mother, I would insist on looking at them before I went to sleep. As we turned into the circular drive leading to the château, everything seemed normal at first. At least the building seemed to be intact, and its blond stone was gleaming in the sun. But when we focused our eyes more closely at the garden, we saw that it was completely ravaged. There were rotting mattresses and disemboweled furniture thrown all about the grounds.

When we got inside the house, after finally getting the door opened, my mother fainted — literally — just fell right down on the floor in the foyer. Time had stood still from the day the Germans left. There were empty wine bottles on the dining room table and dinner plates with decayed scraps still on them. The bathrooms were full of stink. It was so horrible that after we were able to revive my mother, we went outside and sat in the ravaged garden for a long, long time in silence.

My father considered just turning around and going

back to Paris and never coming back, but then he said, *Non*. He said *non* in a way I can still hear today. So it was decided that we would camp out in Tante Marie's little cottage (the subject of so much dispute with Pauline today!), which had been boarded up and apparently just used for storage by the Germans, and so it stank the least.

While my poor parents struggled, I enjoyed myself extremely in those days. My brother and sisters and I were left on our own most of the time and we were like wild Indians, playing our elaborate games.

One day my brother and I were wandering through the *parc*, and we came upon these large holes in the ground (they were in the vineyards). We were very excited by our discovery, and over several days we began an elaborate game of hiding out in the holes, bringing "supplies" from the house each morning, which we would need if "lost in the forest." When my father eventually discovered what we were doing, he became volcanically angry. He grabbed us by the back of our clothes and pulled us up to the house. We were not allowed to leave our rooms for days. I did not understand why he was so angry until many years later. Apparently the "holes" we were playing in were where the Germans had positioned their machine guns.

In any case, my stressed father and mother worked very hard to make the house habitable. So many people from the village came and helped, including, I remember now, M. Ver. But as you know, the house never fully returned to its glory days, and it was years before we could feel that the stink of war had left.

I won't be back home until next Friday. I must help Yvette deal with our apartment here and boring tax matters. Also, I have a very important lead for my Mme. de Maintenon book, and I am very excited by it. There are, perhaps, perhaps, I hope, I hope, some letters still existing from their correspondence when Mme. de M. was at the spa at Barèges. Did I tell you about that? Until now, it has been believed that she destroyed all the letters from that period. Mme. de M. was caretaker of the king's illegitimate son and she took the chronically ill boy to the spa for a cure. It was their correspondence during that difficult time that apparently fired and then sealed their love for each other. So, if true, this would be a great discovery.

Meanwhile, I am seeing a few old friends in the evenings. I still have a great deal of affection for them, and they treat me wonderfully, but I no longer have much interest in what consumes them: constant gossip about this one and that one, and it has little fascination for me now.

A hug to you, and a hug to Marcelline,
Catherine

Mas La Viguerie

Dear Mom,

Well, push came to shove with Marcelline today. If only Marce and I could continue as we have, at least for another year. I feel it's too soon to make a decision. I tried to be as diplomatic as possible, but of course I said all the wrong things. I said that she could move in with me, but then I said we would have to take it one day at a time. We shouldn't see it as absolutely permanent. We both could decide to part at any time. I said, I said, I said, and I said . . . and it was a complete disaster. Clearly I was not giving her the answers she wanted. She curled up in a chair and turned her back to me. Marce, I pleaded, come on, but she refused to talk to me. Marce, please, I have an appointment at my gallery, come with me, I don't want to leave it this way.

I finally gave up and was outside starting my car when she came to the door and shouted out that she was on her way to Paris.

Great.

Your son, Tim

Marcelline Becaze, Paris

Dear Tim,

Oh, my love, I am so ashamed for my behavior, yet again "flying off the handle," as you call it. But I became so agitated during our conversation that I couldn't control my reactions. I didn't even stop to get my clothes, I just drove up to Paris. I am staying with my cousin, René. I am calm now and I can think only of you.

Oh, my dear Tim, I hate it when we can't find a way to communicate. It is so frustrating to me. It upsets me to be seen as someone who is pushing for something that you don't want. I have told you that I am willing to be patient. Would I like children? Of course. Wouldn't you? But I am not in any great hurry. We can wait for the right time.

But for some reason, you do not trust me to do the right thing. We have so much that is right with each other. What is not exactly right, we can work on, or move to the side. I know that sometimes I get carried away with my feelings, and I am trying to get better. But you must trust me.

I miss you so much and kiss you tenderly,

M.

Mas La Viguerie

Dear Marce,

I was very happy to get your letter. Please try to have some fun in Paris and not worry too much. Somehow things will get sorted out. I wish I could give you the exact answer you want. You say that children are not an issue, at least not now, that we can wait and see. But are you just saying what you think I want to hear? Honestly, I don't think you are someone who can just live with a man, or who ought to. During the time spent with your family, I could feel their disapproval of our relationship even though they were very generous and friendly to me.

I really think that Americans have an image of French-women that is a total fantasy. The pull of society here — to marry, to have children — is fierce. This is what I find all around me. I can see that a married woman has a special status. Look at the unspoken power given to Pauline LeDuc that comes from being the married one of the three sisters.

Sometimes I think that there are two Marcellines — the one full of big plans and enthusiasms, and the other that is consumed with worry about her future.

I really miss you, too.

Love,
Tim

Mas La Viguerie

Dear Mom,

The weather today matches my mood: a black sky with slashing rain and crackling thunder. My road is one big mud puddle; I don't dare take the *deux-chevaux* out, so I'm stuck in the house. And if that isn't bad enough, my fireplace got stopped up somehow and smoke poured in and stank up the place.

Ever since Marcelline decided to take off for Paris, I have been getting more and more anxious. Despite how difficult it became between us recently, I am very attached to her. I miss our sweet routines, I miss the delicious food, I miss (let me put it this way) our intense physicality. Honestly, when we are just at home together, *à deux,* we are quite comfortable. She is full of little jokes and fun, but as soon as we venture into the "outside world," friction and dissonance can flood in. We can't quite form an "outside" way of being together. Does this make sense? Marcelline is a good person, but wracked with her own "issues," as they say in the States.

Catherine has put up with my moaning. One of the problems has been that Marcelline couldn't seem to share my friendship with Catherine. I never exclude her from anything, she is always invited along with me, and Catherine is very welcoming to her. But she is always carrying a little black cloud over her head when we are at the château for dinner.

A few days ago, Catherine asked me if I would drive her to see a friend of hers in a small town about twenty miles from here. It was her friend's birthday; her car was in for repairs, and she wanted to deliver a present. She said the trip would help take my mind off my problems. She said she had a surprise for me there and that I should try to keep an open mind. Needless to say, this was quite intriguing.

We had the best drive over to St.-Pierre-Célé. We laughed

and laughed over everything, I can't remember what . . . champagne laughter, Catherine calls it, just bubbles and bubbles, and afterward you can't remember what it was about. Intoxicating.

She took me first to a small church in the village square. In a niche next to the altar was a large gold statue of the Virgin in a very uncharacteristic pose; that is, leaning down as if whispering to someone. Catherine said that it commemorated what happened forty years ago when the Virgin appeared to a young girl and her brother. Apparently the Church has not yet formally recognized the miracle — never speedy, the Catholic Church — but the miracle is accepted by the town and church hierarchy, and every December 1, there is a celebration to which thousands show up. Not quite Lourdes, but let's say in the second tier of Virgin miracles.

Later we stopped in a tiny café for lunch, where we met up with Catherine's friend Josette, the birthday girl. She is about fifty years old, with a sweet but grave manner, much like a nun, I thought immediately. She and Catherine have known each other for years and are clearly fond of each other. As we ate a very nice lunch of *quenelles* with rice (one of only two dishes on the lunch menu), Catherine and Josette chatted animatedly, and I stayed focused on the food. These were my first *quenelles*. I am definitely getting a lot more adventurous with my eating, as before I just would have had the *steak-frites,* the other choice. Anyway, at some point Josette began to talk in a worried way. I heard *archevêque, j'attend, le miracle, something, something,* and as they continued talking it suddenly dawned on me that she was the little girl in the church who had seen the Virgin!

I was so stunned that my plate of *quenelles* landed on the floor. Catherine looked over slyly when she saw the recognition on my face. On the way back home, she told me more about the miracle. Apparently Josette and her brother stopped in the church before going to school. Josette's leg was hurting her and she was having trouble walking. As they reached the altar, the Virgin appeared in a bright light and leaned over to speak to them. Straight from seeing the Virgin, they hurried to their school, and as Josette ran she realized that her leg was no longer painful. Obviously, this phenomenon was no minor occurrence in a tiny village and by the end of the week the church was crowded with townspeople. But it turned out that only the children could see the Virgin. So on Sunday, the girl asked the Virgin to give the people a sign to prove that she wasn't just a little troublemaker. Suddenly a huge ray of light filled the church. *Voilà.* The proof. QED. I asked Catherine the obvious question: Maybe it was the sun crossing the windows? Oh no, she said, it was December and the sun was too low in the sky for that. Then she gave me her best Mona Lisa smile. I don't know what to think about it all. But I have to admit there was something otherworldly about Josette.

Tim

280 West 73d Street, New York

Dear Tim,

I think you're falling under some kind of spell over there. What a remarkable story! When I made a big deal about an encounter with the Virgin Mary when buying the mattress, I was only kidding! You always seemed such a deep skeptic about religion, but that didn't come across at all in your letter. Maybe it was a hot day and you got heat stroke.

I am sorry to hear about the recent stresses with Marcelline. But I can't say I'm completely surprised. If I've learned anything in this life, it is that a romantic situation never remains in stasis. It always evolves for better or for worse, whether we like it or not.

Your Mom

Hôtel des Voyageurs

Dear Mom and Dad,

Brian and I took off on our bike trip today and not a minute too soon. When I put the pedal to the metal, I felt released from the stresses of the last couple of months.

The great thing about biking in the Lot Valley is that with each new bend in the road a brand-new eye-popping vista suddenly appears: the champagne-colored limestone *causses* are the stars of this landscape, then gently rolling hills as far as the eye can see, then ancient stone farmhouses mostly abandoned and covered with lichen, with the slanty roofs of the region, then hedgerows hundreds of years old, then white cattle standing stock-still in a green field. After all the recent emotional Sturm und Drang, I was reminded of why I came to live here in the first place.

I'm writing this letter from the aptly named Hôtel des Voyageurs, having done only twenty-five kilometers today. It's ten P.M. now, and Brian is snoring in the other bed. I put a lot of effort into planning our trip and had a lot of fun doing it. I got Brian outfitted with a super French bike with all the latest bells and whistles, oversized panniers, a Gore-Tex rainsuit, the works. Brian looked like the real deal, but he got off to a shaky start, as it was obvious right away that his conditioning was not what it should have been for a trip of this kind. There are lots of nice flat runs along the riverbeds, but then suddenly out of nowhere there is a steep climb, and one of them nearly killed Brian. So we had to stop a lot, which threw my planning off, and I had to rearrange the hotel stay. The weather had started out great in the A.M. with clear skies and little wind, but by four P.M. the wind was whipping up and the sky got very threatening. We got into the hotel about six P.M., just in time, as it started to pour buckets as we were carrying our bicycles into the hotel lobby.

Brian was really bushed from the ride, and he barely made it into the dining room for dinner. We sat at a long table with the other hotel guests, eight in all. The meal started with a garlic soup (a local specialty, which I loved), and moved on to duck with bitter oranges and a walnut torte for dessert. Brian, though tired, was starving and ate everything put in front of him, but he whispered to me during the meal that the food was a "little weird." Needless to say, this made me not a little bit worried for the rest of the trip.

Tomorrow I hope to make up more time. With luck, we'll make it as far as Millau and stay there overnight.

Your son

St.-Tropez

Dear Mom,

Well, here we are in lovely St.-Tropez, reputed playground of the rich and famous. After Brian and I put our bikes on a train in Montpelier, we arrived in St.-Raphaël on Sunday afternoon. From there, we took an extremely expensive taxi to St.-Tropez. I'll pay, I'll pay, let's just do it, Brian said.

Brian lasted exactly four days on the *vélo* trip. Day two went a little better than day one and we were lucky with the weather. Brian was very sore, but he gritted it out and we made it to Millau before dark. We stayed in a just okay hotel in the center of town with just okay food, which didn't matter much, as we both crashed from the exertion of making up time. On day three we headed to the famous Les Gorges du Tarn, the number one box office attraction of the trip. The Tarn River cuts a spectacularly high gorge through the limestone *causse*, and it took only millions of years of wear and tear on the limestone to accomplish this feat!

We had a surprisingly easy ride around it, no nasty climbs, giving Brian a welcome breather. We stopped to cool our rims at Point Sublime (name well taken), where the view is at its most breathtaking, and even Brian, who usually has been too stressed out from handling his bike to get excited about scenery, recognized that here was something worth noticing. We stayed that night in the town of St.-Chely-du-Tarn, in the Auberge de la Cascade. This very comfortable and charming hotel was not, however, grand enough for Brian, as obviously at some point during the last year Brian's taste for luxury rapidly accelerated. You wouldn't believe how this guy lived in that tiny apartment in Cambridge.

Late that night we sat out by the hotel's pool, on the edge of a cliff overlooking the Tarn. The night sky was overwhelmingly gorgeous, but Brian was on his cell phone for two hours, and it didn't occur to him that I might want to relax and not listen to a lot of loud blather about some insurance company client who was "busting his chops."

I tried to talk him into spending the next day kayaking down the Tarn, but he wasn't interested. By day four, Brian was seriously flagging. Around noon, we hit a real downpour that came out of nowhere, just as we were heading into a tunnel. When we came out the other side, the rain was coming straight at us. Brian hit something in the road and went down hard. He wasn't hurt and we quickly scrambled for cover to wait the rain out. But the fall seemed to suck away what was left of his energy, and that night he chose to abort our mission. The next morning we headed straight to Montpelier.

So the good news is that I haven't been thinking of my "relationship" situation. The bad news is that Brian and I aren't getting along worth spit. Brian, my best friend in college, is now a complete alien to me. We pretty much disagreed on everything. He constantly questioned my scheduling, what time we should leave in the morning, where we should stop on the road, the hotel (never good enough), when we should eat, what we should eat, and on and on. Brian is not a foodnik, to put it mildly. Picking up a delicious lunch of homemade *saucisson*, a fresh baguette, goat cheese, fruit, and then eating it looking out on a gorgeous field of red poppies had zero appeal for him. I swear that he was pissed off that there were no Burger Kings along the route.

Brian arranged for us to stay here in St.-Trop with a few colleagues from his consulting firm. (Did Brian plan all along to accelerate our getting here? I am deeply suspicious.) The guys rented a house for two weeks of partying. They call it blowing off steam, but it's more like toxic fumes. A lot of asshole comments about France. Their favorite joke is to make froggy sounds — *gribic, gribic* — after any encounter with a Frenchman. I have to keep my mouth shut, and it isn't easy. Brian is as bad as the rest of them. Their big deal of the day is going down to the old port in the early afternoon, where they throw a big net over the cafés, and in the evening a whole flock of girls show up for the party!

This happens every night. The girls are very easy on the eyes, but the whole scene makes me crazy. One night — having floated into a very weird frame of mind — I got the sudden flash that maybe I would have a major kismet moment and meet "the right woman," thereby solving all my problems. So *just* as I'm thinking this, a beautiful woman walks straight over to me and introduces herself. She has long brown hair down her back, gorgeous green eyes, a great toned body, and she is an artist with a loft in SoHo. I thought: artist, SoHo loft, New York. Maybe we have a lot in common. Susan (I didn't get her last name) and I went outside and sat down on the terrace ledge, which looks out on a garden that is overrun with masses of lavender, filling the air with an exquisite scent. It was a super night. At this time of year in the south, the sky gets dark very late, and there is a very long twilight of soft, sweet air and a white-gray light. I've recently been trying to get this unique quality into my drawings, but so far I haven't succeeded.

Susan said she was staying in the best hotel in town, which didn't live up to its billing. I mean, Are they kidding or what, she said, my shower is a travesty. She had arrived over a week ago, needing to chill, get into another "head space," after a really intense year. So I asked the not very imaginative but obvious question: What did she think of the south of France? But her head was obviously still back in her New York space, and she proceeded to tell me about her problems with her art dealer — who, she emphasized, owns the top, top gallery in SoHo and who had finally realized what a great artist she is. She recited from memory her latest reviews in *Art News,* and she gave me a guided tour through what *other* artists thought about her work. I had brought a bottle of wine down to the terrace with us, and as she was doing all the talking, I kept sipping away, nodding along, and managed to finish the bottle all by myself. I don't think I said a single word, except inwardly to myself: forget this! Darkness fell in more ways than one, and I left her on the terrace, where she might still be talking to her best audience . . . herself.

I suppose I could just leave the party-hardy house and go home, but I'm not quite ready. I had planned to return home on August 27 and I'm sticking with this date. I am spending my days going to the beach, walking in the hills, sketching a little, but I am still carrying around my anxiety. I am driven somehow to settle the "female" question. I am obsessed with what to do about Marcelline. But it goes deeper than that. She's not the only one obsessing about the future, if I'm honest with myself.

Tim

St.-Tropez

Dear Catherine,

I am writing to you from St.-Tropez. My friend Brian and I lasted four days on our bike trip, and we are now staying in a rented house here with colleagues from his business. I won't bother you with all the reasons why we are now in St.-Tropez, but suffice it to say a bike trip with my friend Brian was not one of my best ideas. I can't be the first person who fantasized about the perfect trip and then was disappointed. When I see you in person I can fill you in on the more hilarious moments, which will be more fun for both of us.

I thought a vacation would put me into a different frame of mind. I thought I could just get away and have pure fun, fun, fun. But the people in this house are driving me crazy. I can't seem to find a way to talk to them. And despite all attempts on my part to put aside my critical assessments, I can't stop thinking that they are just playing at life . . . which is another way of saying that they are driving me crazy. And the person I was closest to in high school and all through college is now a virtual stranger to me.

Here is one of life's really cruel tricks: I think young minds take it for granted that a friendship will last forever, an illusion that may be necessary at the time. As we move on with our own lives, we can lose friends we considered absolutely crucial — and in ways that can be stunningly abrupt and brutal for our psyches. In any case, Brian is gone from my life. Just like that. After this trip, I will probably never talk to him again.

In the ongoing mythos of our friendship, it was a given that Brian was the risk-taker and I was just slowly feeling my way along in life. He was always full of bravado: I'm going to do this, I'm going to do that, just watch my smoke, no one can stop me. The more I think about it, the more I've come to the conclusion that somewhere in their early twenties, people make the *internal* decision to be either a risk-taker or to play it safe. They look out at the vast landscape that looms before them and they make a choice to grab life by the horns or to shrink back and play it safe. The results of this decision don't become obvious immediately because of the masks we wear. But by the mid-thirties, the results are in. It's now clear to me that Brian is not even remotely a risk-taker. Brian made the choice, probably at least ten years ago, to play it safe. He's now slipped into the safety of Mr. Corporate Business Man, a role he once vehemently rejected. I would find this revelation a lot more interesting if it didn't depress me so much.

I really care about Marcelline and like being with her, but I worry about the long term. I realize that it is difficult for one person to satisfy all my needs in life, but I think the question is, How much am I willing to give up for the partnership? I arrived in France a little over two years ago, which hasn't been enough time to get my bearings. I want the pleasure of Marcelline's company, but I want to keep my options open about how to spend the rest of my life. With Marcelline, so many subjects are off-limits. She isn't interested in intellectual arguments, for whatever reasons (either her insecurities, or she just doesn't want to "go there," as they say in the United States).

Is this a "guy thing"? as they also say in the States. Just a man taking what he wants without considering the feelings of the woman? For Marce (and obviously she doesn't say so), I am the villain in this piece. I am resisting the natural course of events, which is to get married. But then why do I experience *her* as ruthless?

I am thinking that you are my best friend. Is this crazy? With you, I have a real meeting of minds. Even though we don't always agree, we can agree on what is important to be discussed. Anything and everything is on the table. I am so very grateful for our friendship.

Your friend, Tim

Rue de Varenne, Paris

Dear Tim,

Your letter touched me deeply. I am happy and honored to be your best friend, but, please forgive me, I think "best friend" is an American concept. In truth, it is very easy for me to listen to you. I'm convinced that our talks have been more helpful to me than to you. Mme. de M.'s most famous quotation is: "The true way to soften one's troubles is to solace those of others."

Your friend Marcelline is a very serious and good girl. She is the eldest daughter, and in France this counts a great deal. I believe that Marcelline is in a very needy phase. She wants to form a family! This is instinctual and not at all blameworthy. When we are young, our selfish behavior can't be seen as horrible. It is quite natural, it is how we rise up in the world.

In our twenties and into our thirties, we are striving to secure a place for ourselves in the world. When I was living in Paris in the sixties, I met many men who said they loved me madly and wanted to marry me immediately! But what was I really to them, except an object of their need. Did they know me at all? But in fact, I had my own needs. It was difficult to be a woman out in society without a male escort, so I was happy to have their attention. But when I would protest that I wasn't ready to marry, some would claim that I was just using them or, more cuttingly, that I was cold.

What I have discovered over time is how ruthless we all are in the name of love. Love is what we are all about, we claim. I love you, we say. But then we complain, You are not giving me what I want! We want attention. We want what we want. In truth, life is a negotiation — in the best and worst sense.

You need to be gentle with Marcelline and try to understand. But the more difficult thing is to decide what you want for yourself.

As we get older, I think we begin to realize that the antidote to our anxieties about keeping love in our lives is to concentrate on *giving*. The old cliché that giving love is better than receiving it is completely true, but it's very difficult to learn this. *Giving* annihilates the ruthlessness intrinsic in trying to get our needs met and, paradoxically, almost always ends up bringing us what we wanted in the first place! I know this to be absolutely true, but, sad to say, I have not always been a practitioner.

Please forgive me, I'm so sorry for going on and on, but what I appreciate about you is that you are so receptive to all kinds of ideas. You roll them around in your mind and respond in a pure way. I enjoy it so much, and I have come to realize how thirsty I have been for lively discussions. After being in your company, I often feel *inquiète* . . . but not in a bad way, please don't misunderstand. Sometimes very late at night, when I am just falling asleep, I actually can imagine frozen pieces of myself falling away. As difficult as these sensations are, I am grateful for them. I know that in so many ways I had begun to believe my life would never change, except in the inexorable way of waiting for death. But again, please forgive me for going on in this way. I must stop writing now, as I'm getting morbid and silly.

I am looking forward to your return.

Affectionately,
Catherine

Mas La Viguerie

Dear Holly,

I'm writing to you because you are the only person I can trust with this stuff. You absolutely cannot say a word to Mom and Dad, as I am trying to figure out what to do — and whatever I figure out, I would like to tell them about it myself.

After I got back from my road trip with Brian, I was really messed up, completely tied up in knots. I can't remember ever being like this. The bike trip was supposed to be a relaxing time, but I came back feeling worse than when I left.

The morning after I arrived home, Marcelline showed up with an armload of packages. She was talking a mile a minute. She had bought *so* many beautiful things in Paris . . . Look at this shirt I found for you, from the *best* men's store in Paris . . . and the most exquisite candlesticks, late-nineteenth century, they will look perfect on the dining table. She was full of energy, but I could sense her tension underneath. She said she had got an extension on her lease and didn't need to move out for another month. She claimed that she was perfectly fine and that she had had the best, best time in Paris. She told me that she had come to realize that I was absolutely right, we should take it one day at a time, and she was completely comfortable with that.

I was really happy to see her, but I wanted to shake her:

Marce, please don't do this. Don't tell me what you think I want to hear! She gave me a strange and scared look, but didn't answer. My energy sank and I felt an unfamiliar disconnected feeling between us. But then I censored myself: Cool down, cool down, maybe she's just overanxious. After all, you've been apart for several weeks. The feeling buzzing in your brain will go away. We kissed a lot, hugged a lot, and then we fell into bed. But as much as we were both willing, we were trying too hard, and it was, oh never mind, I think you can figure it out.

A few days later, I went over to Catherine's to work in her mother's old painting studio. It was late afternoon when I got there, but Catherine was not painting in the garden, as she usually is at that hour. I thought about going up to the house to find her, but I stopped myself, I'm not sure why.

I steeled myself to go into the studio. Then I tried to settle myself at my easel, but it was hard to focus. The drawings I had done most recently — and had felt very good about — looked horribly primitive, beyond redemption. I could hardly breathe, I was so depressed by them. I sat there doing nothing for a long while. Mostly I rearranged canvases, cleaned up a lot, and beat myself up for my obvious lack of talent.

As I was leaving the studio, Catherine waved to me from the terrace. She called out that she had seen me arrive, wanted to say hello immediately, but that she was so distracted with house business that she couldn't pull herself away from it. Please, please, stay for a drink, isn't the garden ravishing at this time of day, so lovely, so lovely, please stay.

She brought out a tray with a bottle of Lillet and water. We sat silently for some time, sipping our drinks, but before I knew it, I was spilling my guts out about Marcelline. It was the same old stuff, but I couldn't help myself.

I suddenly looked over at Catherine, having realized I had probably been ranting on for a very long time. She was sitting very still, her head lowered, her hands in her lap. I got a flash of paranoia that she was tired of hearing all my moaning and was completely bored with me. I clammed up and just kept staring at her. After what seemed like hours, she finally lifted her head and turned to look over at me. The air stopped moving, I swear it. I couldn't focus my eyes. "If only I were younger," she said.

That was all she said. But now it can't be taken back and it has changed everything.

I'll write again as soon as I can, but needless to say it's a little hard to concentrate right now, and please, please, not a word yet to Mom and Dad.

Tim

Château de la Rive

My dearest Yvette,

Please don't be shocked by what I am about to tell you. I am just myself absorbing the enormity of what has happened. I could not have imagined myself doing something like this in a million years.

I know you have seen the great sympathy between Tim and myself, and you've even teased me about it. Tim says that you once said to him that he and I got along so well, we were like an old married couple. And it's true. From our very first meeting, we established an easy friendship, a very welcome one for me after the difficult years when Maman was so ill, and the lonely years that followed her death.

Over the last several months, Tim was in a lot of turmoil over his relationship with Marcelline. I tried to give him the most detached kind of advice, but more and more my heart wasn't in it. Pauline, in her usual way, had very strong opinions about Marcelline and Tim being together. One day she and I were talking, and she suddenly announced that I absolutely must tell Tim that Marcelline was wrong for him. She will ruin his life if he marries her, she insisted. I said, Pauline, please, I can't do that, it is not our business to interfere in Tim's life in that way. And yet a part of me agreed that a marriage with Marcelline was probably ill-fated. Pauline was adamant. You must tell him. Pauline, calm down, calm down, I kept saying, and then I just went out into the garden, as I usually do when she gets so insistent and won't stop talking.

In July, Tim left on a bicycle trip with a friend from America and was gone for almost four weeks. Days before he was scheduled to leave, I began to notice a strange agitation in myself. At one point, I was actually about to ask him why such a long trip but quickly stopped myself, as I thought, Is this *really* any of my business? During the period that he was away, I had a great deal of difficulty concentrating on my painting. I found myself worrying about where he was. And then I began to have a growing fear that I would lose him. At first, I berated myself for being a silly goose. What did I mean, "Lose him"? I didn't *have* him. It seemed so irrational and reminded me of feelings I had had at the beginning of my relationship with Bertrand. You are not yourself, I kept thinking. But what became very clear was how much Tim's person had merged into my inner world and my daily life here.

He had told me he would be back home on August 27. I therefore somehow had fixed in my mind that he would come to paint at the studio the next day. But he didn't arrive, and I had to stop myself from going to see him at his farm or calling him. Then two days later, he showed up in the afternoon to paint, and despite being relieved I was actually fearful of going outside to see him. I waited until he was about to leave and then I got up my courage and called out to him from the house to come for a drink on the terrace.

At first, he began describing his biking trip and his many disappointments with the American friend he traveled with, but before long his conversation turned to Marcelline. It was clear that he was now in even more agony over making a decision about living with her. And gradually his worry over Marcelline turned to despairing that there was probably no woman in the world that was right for him. And, God help me, out of my mouth came the words, "If only I were younger . . ."

He looked startled, but then his face lit up and I saw immediately that he returned the feeling.

We sat together for a long time, holding hands tightly, mostly without speaking, our feelings igniting the air around us. It is fair to say that we both realized — or, more accurately — acknowledged the underlying truth of the past months . . . that we had fallen in love with each other.

After this fateful conversation, I floated in our garden for what seemed like hours, I was in such a helium state. A full moon was directly overhead and our cedar tree looked like a giant monster looking down at me. Somehow I got into the house and floated to my bedroom and then threw myself heavily down on the bed. I was so full of feeling, I actually thought about tying myself down, afraid I would rise up to the ceiling during the night!

I finally managed to fall asleep, but in the early morning I woke up suddenly — literally threw myself bolt upright. Every possible fear or negative thought had entered my sleep: What have I done? What have I done to Tim? I felt wretchedly selfish, as I kept thinking, He is still so young. I couldn't bear it if being with me damaged him in any way. I felt overwhelmed with guilt. Why didn't I just keep quiet? What had possessed me? I was crazy to think that we could actually be together in some way. I decided that I must tell him immediately that it was all a mistake, just a moment of overexcitement. It would be terribly embarrassing for me, but it had to be done.

As I drove over to his farm, I couldn't remember ever being in such a nervous state. When I pulled up to his farmhouse, he was standing outside the front door and I nearly ran into him, forgetting to put my foot on the brake. But as soon as I managed to get out of the car — and before I could say a word — we just fell into each other's arms, and from that moment we immediately resumed being our comfortable selves with each other. There was not a second of embarrassment, something I had been preparing myself for. Since then we have been meeting every day, and now our feelings for each other cannot be put aside.

I will anxiously await some word from you. You know how I rely on your good sense.

Catsu

Rue de Varenne, Paris

Chère Catsu,

I am not altogether surprised by your letter. A few months ago, I was playing the piano in the château salon, and at some point, in an abstracted frame of mind (you know how I am), I drifted over to the window and was looking out onto the *parc*. In the midst of my reverie, my eyes came upon you and Tim sitting on the bench by the *orangerie*.

It was quite late in the afternoon and it wasn't the first time I had seen you both out there after your respective painting sessions, so I'm not sure exactly what was different that evening, but an electric shock ran through me.

The two of you were sitting very close together, your foreheads nearly touching, and it came to me that you looked like lovers. I was reminded of a sculpture, or a very stylized painting. I remember that a distinct feeling of worry came over me, but I quickly put it out of my mind. Just my imagination, the light, the distance, and so on.

You know I only want you to be happy, that it is not in my nature to interfere with what others do. I have come to understand that life takes us down many unexpected paths. How we imagined we would end up when we were young and naive is rarely the way our lives turn out. This has been true for both of us. I certainly didn't expect to be living entirely on my own in Paris, without family or children. So what fills your soul at this time of your life is something you should reach for without question. God has unique ways of blessing us.

Googoo

Park Slope, Brooklyn

Dear Bro,

I can't believe you! Younger Sister finally has the event of childbirth to rival anything in Older Brother's arsenal, and what does he come up with: *Le grand amour* with Mlle. Benoir! You always knew how to top me.

But seriously, my big news, if you have a minute, is that I have given birth to your niece, Tara. She weighed eight pounds, nine ounces, a big, beautiful girl. Despite all my initial ambivalence, I am so happy that I pushed myself to have this baby now. Brad wanted it so much, and I had to honor his feelings if I was to stay in a marriage with him. It's odd, but I kept thinking I would lose myself — pregnancy seemed to me like "free-fall" — and that I had to surrender, which filled me with deep dread. After an initial period of shell shock, the so-called surrender to childbirth has paradoxically made me feel amazingly more complete.

Anyway, you are one lucky guy that I was so occupied in my own business that I didn't call Mom right away after getting your letter. You know I was never good at keeping secrets! It doesn't surprise me that you would do something that didn't follow a strict code of normal behavior. But I am still just blown away. I had begun to develop a very romantic notion of Catherine . . . so beautiful, so aristocratic, so sophisticated. But not as my brother's girlfriend! I know she is an "older woman," but she's not just any older woman. Come on. Excuse me, I don't mean to be rude, but what does she see in you? On the other hand, why would you choose her? Yes, I know you have a strong interest in art in common, but culturally you still seem a million miles apart. Help!

Holly, mother of Tara

Mas La Viguerie

Dear Holly,

On its way to you by separate post is a drawing of Château de la Rive. It is my very modest gift to baby Tara from her uncle Tim. I am flat-out happy for you and really wish I could make a trip back home to see my niece (keep sending those gorgeous photos), but hopefully I (or we?) will be able to get to New York next year.

Please hold out a little longer on saying anything to the folks about Catherine and me. I just can't bring myself to call them. It's too big a thing to blurt out over the phone. So I've been composing a letter and, as you can imagine, it's not the easiest letter I've ever written.

No one could be more surprised than I am by what has happened. It's true that on the surface Catherine and I seem a very unlikely pairing, but you have to understand that the buildup of feelings between us was very gradual. After being treated so welcomingly by the whole Benoir family, particularly her sister Pauline, over time I started to see more and more of Catherine, and there began a slow entwining of our daily lives. I started going over for dinner or lunch several times a week. Soon we began checking in with each other almost every day, and I started painting in her mother's old studio, which is a wonderful space and has the best possible light.

The more time we spent together, the more our strong affinities became obvious, and our outer differences melted away. Even more importantly, my admiration for her kept growing and our conversations about painting became very important to me. Even our disagreements about technique were extremely energizing for my work.

When I would then see Marcelline in the evenings, conversation would become forced, as Marce resisted listening to anything about Catherine, and I would feel heavily brought down to earth. So part of my anguish over what to do about my relationship with Marcelline was always the unassailable fact that if we began living together I would almost certainly have to give up my friendship with Catherine. And this sacrifice began to feel impossible: I did not want to lose her.

Since our big moment of recognition, Catherine and I have been spending a lot of time agonizing over how we are going to make a life together. And on top of this, there is my double agony over facing Marcelline!

When Marce called for an explanation as to why she hadn't heard from me, I behaved like any craven male. I said, No, no, no, of course I'm not avoiding you, I'm just so crazy-busy since I got back, I've got a horrible cold, hack, hack, hack, but I'm sure I'll be better tomorrow, let me call you. Completely disgusting behavior, but I justified it by telling myself I couldn't possibly tell her the truth over the phone. I would have to write a letter, which of course I kept putting off.

Then yesterday, Marce arrived in the afternoon without warning. She said that she *really, really* had to have some answers. And when I froze in my tracks and went mute, she became, of course, completely disgusted in the name of all females since the beginning of time with the pathetic communication skills of males. So she sucked in her breath, whipped around, and went stalking off toward the sheep barn to calm down. Before I could relish this temporary relief from a head-on confrontation, Catherine's car suddenly pulled into the drive!

Catherine, full of energy, came forward to hug me . . . and at this precise moment, Marcelline emerged from behind the sheep barn. Imagine this scene in slow motion: Marcelline throws her head backward, I instinctively lurch forward but immediately retreat backward, and Catherine, quickly realizing the import of what is happening, tries to save the moment by walking calmly into the house with a basket of food. Needless to say, the embrace between Catherine and myself was unmistakable in its feeling, imbedding a stake in Marcelline's heart, and she ran for her car.

Remember my big theory — spouted endlessly at family dinners — that the most important things in life occur in the Unsaid? Well, none of the protagonists in this drama uttered a *single word*, but everything changed in that moment.

The next day Marcelline showed up with a typed, very lawyerly list of things that belonged to her. As soon as I opened the door, she blasted in saying she had *absolutely nothing* to say to me, and then proceeded to render me nearly prostrate with her avalanche of words: I had never had any feeling for her, I was just using her, she was never good enough for me, I was a complete fraud, on the alert for a better opportunity, sucking up to those rich phony Benoirs, and that poor old-maid sister, Catherine, I pity her, she doesn't know that I am just after her money.

I didn't even try to defend myself. Whatever I said would sound so pathetic, like, I didn't mean to hurt you. And, honestly, who could blame her for her outrage. The situation certainly looks very bad, and she is going to hate me for a long time, probably forever. Everything she asked for from the house, I gave her, including the antique candlesticks she brought back from Paris. She said I had accepted this gift under false pretenses, and *Mademoiselle* has plenty of candlesticks, she was sure, gouging a deep wound into my flesh. Then she stormed out. She didn't need her car to leave. She probably could have gotten as far as Paris on sheer fury.

What a drama your brother has gotten himself into. This is the same brother who I'm sure you'll remember was always first out the door at the sign of even remotely messy emotional stuff.

I keep telling myself to just take it one day at a time.

Love,
Your bro

Château de la Rive

My sweet Tim,

It is late in the afternoon, the sun is a rosy gold, and I am sitting on the terrace attempting to let my thoughts flow out onto this piece of paper. As freely as we can talk to each other, sometimes it is easier to pull up the deeper layers of what's going on in one's mind in a letter.

Pure joy may be running through my veins since we acknowledged our love for each other, but at the same time I now feel more naked to the world. A long personal sadness creates over time a cocoon, a necessary protective cover, and so paradoxically my new happiness has left me feeling terribly exposed.

It was brutal to experience Marcelline's pain so directly yesterday, but it awoke me to what we may be facing in the future. More than just feeling rejected, Marcelline was completely shocked that you would make such an extra-ordinary choice — this old woman over me! — and her whole sense of how the world works was turned upside down. Granted, she always felt insecure around me, but this didn't extend to thinking I would usurp her place.

Love can come at any age. But with this new love of ours, I am suddenly more acutely aware of my own age and the difference in age between us.

I found myself exploring my own feelings about women older than myself when I was Marcelline's age. I remember walking into a grand party with Bertrand and experiencing the glares of women his own age. Now I understand better that women are themselves conditioned by the interest of men in women much younger than themselves. When we are young, we are so full of strut: get out of my way, here I come with the full power of youth. And young love rarely takes into account how finite a love can be. But in the end, life itself is the great equalizer. We all age, as day follows day follows day.

When I think to the future, I honestly don't worry for myself. We can expect that some people will make us the butt of their jokes, but I worry that they will say things about you that are entirely undeserved. I worry that if you stick with me, you will never have children. I try not to think that if only we had met sooner, we could have had children together, but this is silly and pointless. I also worry that in later years you may become burdened with an aging woman.

Would I suffer if we couldn't continue? Of course, overwhelmingly so. But I would survive. Last night, you were full of feeling and insisted that we should get married.

Please think about what this means. It's true that for me, life would be vastly less complicated if we married, but I would never want you to make such a decision just to protect me.

I want you to know that if at any point you feel you cannot continue — for whatever reason — I will never hold you back in any way and will let you go freely.

Love,
Catherine

Mas La Viguerie

Dear Catherine,

I read your letter over and over, and all I can think to say is: What choice do we have?

For my part, I don't feel that loving you is in any way a voluntary act. Could I just say to myself, Okay, enough of this nonsense? Just forget this woman and move on? I could no more do this than I could stop breathing and still think I was alive.

Obviously, we are not a typical couple equation. We don't fit within a statistical norm: you age twenty, me age twenty-two, marrying and having children. We're operating outside societal imperatives for procreation. But so what?

You'll laugh, but last night, like the math guy I once was in my now decidedly "other life," I was sitting at my desk doodling on a piece of paper and I unconsciously slipped into creating an algorithm for our present situation, which is essentially a flow chart, or logical arrangement of all the contributing elements. Once I listed them all, I assigned a numerical value, or weight, to each of them from the set of real whole numbers, positive and negative, depending on their relative merit. For example, the value I assigned to our opposition was −10; then I assigned +10 for the value of our love. I added the numbers up, divided by the number of elements to get an average number, then compared the result to a threshold value of zero. And *voilà!* — and this is hardly serious, obviously highly emotional mathematics (a contradiction in terms) — but the answer is: we should definitely get married.

Please, please put the issue of age into a drawer and don't take it out again. I love you as you are. You are beautiful in every way. You have to be certain of that. Will life change for us along the way? I'm sure it will. Will our different ages be a factor? I'm sure they will. But I'm not going to spend a lot of time thinking about these unknowables.

I plan to enjoy every day with you as if it's our last.

All my love,
Tim

Château de la Rive

Chère Yvette,

What I have to say may seem sudden to you, but after

a great deal of discussion, Tim and I have come to the conclusion that we should marry.

Once we acknowledged our feelings for each other, the overriding question became how to fashion a life together. We quickly realized that if we were to spend time with each other freely, the change in our habits would be immediately noticed, which, as you know, would draw speculation about the changed relationship. As "young at heart" as I think I am, we cannot just begin living together. Nor can we just "run away." No doubt we will be the subject of gossip no matter what we do — I am bracing myself for that — but I hope that at least we can prevent a scandal. We were feeling completely stuck, until we came to see that the solution was to get married.

Yesterday I went to see Père Fleury at the chapel. Poor man, his Parkinson's is acting up. He was sitting in his tiny room as usual, drinking his cup of coffee, and I noticed that his hands were shaking more than ever, and he couldn't stop his wooden leg from rattling against the table. It was unnerving, needless to say.

He was quite amazed by what I had to tell him — and maybe even a little excited, bless him, as it's probably the most surprising news he's had in a long time! I told him that I realized that he might consider the situation unconventional, but he just shrugged and said, *"Ça arrive."* I had to laugh, what a *drôle* little man he is.

He asked if Tim had ever been married, and I said no. Well then, he said, as neither of you has ever been married, there should be no impediment if you decide to make such a union. Then he asked if Tim was a Catholic. Again, I said no. Do you think he would convert? he asked. I said we hadn't discussed it, but I noticed a little more excitement in Père's voice, as he contemplated the possibility of a convert, something that probably hasn't come his way in decades.

I told him that Pauline was in fact the one who had first met Tim, and that it was she who initiated the invitation to our house, so Tim is not at all a stranger to her or her family. They have always gotten along very well, and many pleasurable hours had been spent at the château with Tim joining our family. But of course I realized that the idea of marriage with Tim was something else again, and I said that they will certainly be surprised and possibly even shocked, and here is where I hoped he could come to my assistance. Père Fleury said he could understand my concern, as I was not making the most common alliance, and he would certainly welcome the family members if they came to him for counsel. He said that he realized that many people might not understand that there are those rare individuals on this earth who can experience a higher kind of love.

I tried hard to suppress a laugh and, God help me, I actually said that I wasn't interested in that kind of love. He blushed a bright red and then hastily said he had to begin his preparations for mass.

On the way out, I nearly knocked over Soeur Blanche,

who was obviously listening to our conversation with her ear planted to the door. She scurried away as quickly as possible — for someone over ninety!

I control my emotions by forcing myself to do my everyday things. Painting is out of the question, as I cannot sit still. I have a commission from M. and Mme. Dutelier for a portrait of their daughter, but I have had to tell them I cannot accept now.

But our garden is benefiting greatly from my anxiety. I had been putting off for weeks the tedious work on the rose arbor, but now I've managed to charge through it in two days. And I've been spending a lot of time with Pépé. God truly blessed us the day he took over management of our vineyards. You'll be happy to know that he is very optimistic about the size and quality of this year's grape harvest, so that we are likely to have more income this year, something that will be very welcome.

I hope you will not judge me harshly. Whatever sophistication I may have thought I had has dropped away, and I feel as vulnerable as a kitten. Pauline is due here in two weeks and I am steeling myself for her reaction. I keep telling myself that, after all, it was she who introduced me to Tim, and she has always been wonderful with him.

I embrace you,
Catherine

Rue de Varenne, Paris

Chère Catherine,

My heart is with you no matter what you decide. I do understand how difficult it would be for the two of you to live together outside of marriage.

But I have to say that I worry how Pauline will react. You know how she is. Our brother, do you remember, always felt that if either of us got married, Pauline would suffer. I used to laugh at that. What do you mean? I would say. Of course she wants us to marry, she's always trying to match us up with someone. But the men were always the most impossible choices. Remember how Pauline kept pushing you to marry skinny, gray-faced Charles Thierry, Mr. Bow and Scrape? *"Bonjourbonjourbonjourbonjour,"* he'd say as his head would nearly touch the ground. You kept telling Pauline no, no, no, don't be absurd, but she kept pounding away at it, how rich he was, his family pedigree, don't be a fool. I think I now understand more deeply what lay under what our brother was trying to say.

I miss our brother terribly today, as he always could stem Pauline's force when necessary. So many of our recent difficulties with her at the château could have been easily worked out if Louis had been here to smooth the way. Remember what Maman used to say about Pauline: that she couldn't wait to get older so she could boss everyone around.

With my deep affection, Yvette

Mas La Viguerie

Dear Mom and Dad,

First, some good financial news: Mathilde has gotten me a commission from a very famous abbey called Cure- monte. One of the Benedictine monks happened to be in Villefranche a few months ago and somehow wandered into Mathilde's gallery, where he saw some of my land- scape paintings. Following this stroke of happenstance, I've now been formally asked to create a series of murals for a gallery room that the abbey is in the process of build- ing.

I asked Mathilde to explain that I wouldn't have a clue about doing religious paintings. After a lot of back-and- forth, I was told that the abbey was interested in pure landscapes that would bring a fresh look to the space, not exactly what I expected to be doing as a painter, but really good experience. And pretty good money, which I can definitely use now. I worried about the size of the project, that it was way beyond my abilities, but Catherine said I had to focus on what I *can* do, then push myself to work beyond my present skills. And if it turns out that I will need help, then I can ask for it.

So first I will have to camp at the abbey for at least two weeks to work up my ideas and do preliminary sketches. The Abbaye Curemonte is in the Limousin, about a four- hour drive north of here. I'm looking forward to seeing this part of France, as I read somewhere that it is even more underpopulated than the Lot. Obviously, my kind of place.

And now the *big* news. God knows what you're going to think. You may be upset, I don't know. I have to confess that I have been putting off contacting you, trying to get up my courage, as until today it has been just too intimate a thing to talk about.

You know from my letters that I was struggling for a long time over my relationship with Marcelline and that our situation had come to a head when she had to move out of her house.

You also know from spending time here how important my friendship with Catherine had become. The more I agonized, the more I began to recognize my growing feelings for Catherine, but I just didn't know what to do with them. When I returned from my bike trip, I went to see Catherine and (without going into a lot of personal detail) we simultaneously realized that our friendship had turned into something much deeper, that we had fallen in love with each other.

The day after our moment of revelation, we were both anxious about seeing each other again, but to my complete surprise there was not a second of discomfort between us. Instead, we had a great time talking and joking about the "run-up" to our moment of recognition. She was positive that I would think she was a foolish ninny. I was sure she would just laugh me off. And so on.

So this news may seem extremely sudden to you, but

trust me, we've thought long and hard about it, and we believe that we should get married.

I don't know how Catherine's family will react. Pauline is definitely the wild card. I get along very well with her, she is always charming to me, and I have spent plenty of time around her family, so they know me quite well and are comfortable with me. Pauline's oldest son, Roger, has even become a pal; when he's staying at the château, he shows up to help with my garden; he is a genius with plants. One of Pauline's daughters, Solange, has been particularly kind to me. She and her husband bought several drawings from me recently, and they went overboard in their praise. And all the various grandchildren are a special delight, particularly little Martine-Marie, Solange's eight-year-old, who when she sees me follows me around like a little puppy asking me to draw her something. Some of them actually call me Uncle Tim.

Yes, there is an age difference, but I really don't experience it viscerally in any way when we are together. In fact, the feelings I have for Catherine are distinctly of a different order than any I have ever had for a woman. To be very candid: I have always started with immediate sexual passion with my girlfriends, and then we have had to sort out (sometimes extremely painfully) whether we had anything remotely in common. So I find myself shocked that I've now become a poster boy for an extremely conservative approach to conjugal union.

I'm really grateful that you were able to spend time

here and meet Catherine. Can you imagine if I had announced our engagement without your having met her or been here?

Love, Tim

280 West 73d Street, New York

Dear Tim,

First, I want to say that when we returned from our visit with you, it was mostly about Catherine that I spoke to my friends. I kept bringing out the pictures I took of her at the château, extolling her beauty and bragging that my son had such an extraordinary friend.

So I know firsthand that Catherine is a beautiful woman in every way, and the romantic in me can't help respond to the story of a woman of a "certain age" finding unexpected love with a younger man — and of course I have to be puffed up that she thinks so highly of my son.

So whatever I have to say relating to the two of you forming a union has to do only with its complications and dissonance, the things you might not be taking into consideration yet, in the heat of the moment, so to speak.

What I fear is that you may be idealizing the possibilities of a life with Catherine and not fully considering what problems will undoubtedly arise. Right now, the age difference might not feel daunting. Catherine is vigorous and healthy, and you are both matched in interests and energy. But what about ten years from now? You will still be a relatively young man, but she will be nearing seventy.

Think about how you struggled with your feelings about Marcelline. I wonder if after the storms of the past months with her you are just sailing into a seemingly safe port? Sometimes people make choices just to assuage a lonely life in the country.

The Benoir family is not only Catholic, but as you've told us, Jansenist Catholic. Your father, in his typical way, has been reading up, and he says that Jansenists are well known for their extreme piety, something that I doubt will work in your favor. Don't you think the problems a marriage with you could create for Catherine with her family are a serious consideration, and an unfair burden to put upon her?

As you know, your father had a Jewish father and a nonpracticing Catholic mother, but he was raised Episcopalian (the religion of his grandmother) by his grandparents. I of course had a Jewish mother and a Christian father, both nonpracticing. A complete hodgepodge! The result of our respective upbringings is that neither of us took part in any conventional religious practice. We would like to think that we provided you and Holly with good educations and the basis for making independent judgments about spiritual practice, but you grew up in secular New York, for good or ill. So you may not be fully appreciating all the ramifications of the Benoir family's Catholicism, and therefore underestimating their reaction to your marrying Catherine.

You haven't said how Catherine's personal religious convictions — apart from her family background — come into the picture, that is, the need to sanctify your alliance before God. If this is not an issue, I wonder about your need to marry. Why can't you and Catherine just go on as you are, or find a comfortable way to live together outside marriage?

And what about having children? My grandmother gene is very active these days. Do you want to leave the entire familial burden on Holly? Seriously, I don't mean to presume too much, but even though you may not be thinking about children this minute, what about a few years from now, when you might change your mind? What will you do then?

Your father is equally thrown for a loop by your news, but in his typical way — that classic silent male way of just turning over all emotionally charged situations to the woman — he is just saying, Well, and hmm, and I don't know, and I guess we have to say *something*, why don't you write him, and so on, and he told me to just send you his love and support, but I know that he is as concerned as I am.

Love,
Your Mom

P.S. I suppose I should be thankful that I wasn't a teenage bride. Otherwise your intended would be older than I am!

Mas La Viguerie

Dear Mom,

Thank you for being so honest in your letter. What
you say is very sensible and logical, but in fact there is really no question of Catherine and me just continuing as
we have — whatever that may mean — or living together
without being married.

Everything has changed. As you said yourself in a recent letter, nothing ever stays the same in relationships.
Once Catherine and I acknowledged our feelings for each
other, they couldn't be taken back, and now the have ex-
panded exponentially, and we want to be together as much
as possible. Love happens, and it cannot be undone.

Living together might work if we were in New York,
but not here. And there is really no question of our moving away from here. We talked for, oh, about a minute and
a half about moving to New York, but it's not a real option
for Catherine, and obviously I came here for a reason, so
why would I move back?

Don't get the idea that we are not taking into consideration all the pros and cons of our situation. I did have
some doubt-filled days, but I overcame them very quickly.
Catherine has had a harder time, and has many more
concerns than I do. Actually, we are more concerned for
each other than for ourselves. I worry about how she will
be perceived. Her family has been here for generations.
Cajarc is not New York. So being with me will make her

the subject of gossip. She is concerned that I might at some point want to have children and regret my decision, and that I may be perceived as taking advantage of her, a *parvenu*, as the French would say.

You rightly point out my ambivalent feelings about a marriage with Marcelline, and I myself wondered at the time if I was just resistant to the idea of marriage itself. But with some distance I can see that I was not the right man for her. External pressures on Marcelline to marry and have a family were very intense, and when it came to me she was grasping at straws. The storms you refer to, I realize now, were in large part due to my growing feelings for Catherine — which I didn't know what to do with.

Please don't get the idea that Catherine is pressing me to marry her. It is not like that at all. I was the one to bring up marriage, not just because she is Catholic, but because, as you pointed out yourself, living with me outside of marriage would place an unfair burden on her *vis-à-vis* her family. For her part, she is more concerned about me, about what I theoretically must give up to be with her, and she has already said that we must give each other up if the burden on me becomes insupportable. She is who she is; she can go on and find pleasure and interest in her life.

Here is a terrible confession: I have never seen myself with children. Probably the dreaded shrink we went to for family therapy would say I am too selfish or too narcissistic or too something or other, but I just think the instinct for fatherhood did not come in the box when I was born. Who, ultimately, can say why?

You bring up the question of Catherine's age. Catherine is beautiful — I would have thought beyond-me beautiful — and it's true that at first her age seemed an obstacle. When I first met her, I certainly didn't see her as a potential partner in any sense of the word. And yes, if a question had been posed, I would have said automatically that she was too old for me. She seemed from an inaccessible time and place, another culture, another generation, all that and more. We have had many quite blunt conversations about age. Yes, I'm likely to outlive her. Conversely, I might get hit by a truck tomorrow, and she would be left a widow. Does looking "coldly" at the future mean freezing out the present?

I came here to work as an artist. All the time I trained in math, drawing and painting remained a big part of my life. In fact, the two disciplines complemented each other — that is, until I had to deal with the academic world. Oddly enough, as an artist I have never been attracted by abstraction but by representation, by what I consider *pure* painting. Our overlapping interest in art has played a large part in our coming together. Our mutuality began gradually, building on an immediate visual sympathy, and of course humor, the same little jokes, a similar take on people's character, and, ultimately, despite our surface differences, the same values.

Catherine says that when she first met me, she thought

I was an attractive man, but a bit of a *clochard* because of the way I dressed — hardly a lovely compliment! She certainly didn't think of me as a potential boyfriend. She says now that she realized that she reacted instinctively to the fact that I was not dressed like a man her parents would have approved of or, on further thought, that she would have imagined choosing for herself.

Maybe country life blurs the lines between people more than city life, as I'm sure that if we were both living in Paris, our paths might never have crossed. But looking at it another way, there is a reason we are both here in one of the most rural parts of France and have found each other at a time when we have stripped away our "city" presentations of self. So I guess that the more time Catherine spent with me, the more attractive I became to her, as she obviously stopped looking at my clothes!

People might see our relationship as out of the ordinary, but really it is very simple. It is a matter of wanting to spend all the hours we have on earth with each other — with separate, differentiated spaces, of course — because that is another thing that comes completely naturally to both of us, a respect for each other's separateness. But we want to talk together, eat together, sleep together, make plans together. We just endlessly enjoy being with each other.

I know you may think that I've drunk some strange love potion and have been taken over by a fantasy of miraculous love . . . or on a crass level, am trying to get myself taken care of by attaching myself to a highborn Frenchwoman.

But the simple truth is that as soon as our feelings became clear, it just seemed right. Mundane selfish brute that I've been until now, I am beginning to understand what all those poets were getting at . . . that love brings an ineffable feeling of transcendence. I've come to understand in an *experiential* way that the feeling is pure and irrevocable. We are bound. I can't explain it any better. I have also begun to understand so many things I read in college that I really didn't grasp at the time: you know, what young boys dismiss as all that lovey-dovey stuff. I had a moment of silly collegiate fame for a comedy shtick I worked up based on a spirited denunciation of *Tristan and Isolde,* assigned in a lit class, and to which I had an extreme loathing. A stupid story, I thought, of love potions, dying for love, dying for just an hour together, dying to be together in another life. I got a lot of mileage out of it. I called my riff "Cosmic Superglue." But anyway, enough of that, I don't want to sound completely idiotic.

Catherine said to me that if I ever felt I had to leave her, whatever the reason, she would let me go without a word. I later asked her, But what if we married in the Catholic Church? Wouldn't a divorce be a problem for you? Well, she said, since I can't imagine marrying again, you would need only to talk to my sister Pauline. She has wonderful connections in the Church hierarchy, and she could easily get us an annulment.

We had a big laugh and we both agreed that in the end, life requires continual acts of bravery. How many people stay in the miserable present because they are afraid of the consequences of change? So I hope you will be in our corner.

With love,
Tim

Mas La Viguerie

Dear Mom and Dad,

All hell broke loose yesterday.

Pauline showed up at the château with an army of her daughters and sons and assorted spouses behind her. Catherine was in the kitchen having tea and talking to Bette, the *femme de ménage,* when the door swung open and Pauline whipped right up, like a Fury from Greek myth, and screamed into Catherine's face that she had Alzheimer's!

Catherine had been gearing up to tell Pauline about us but was having difficulty settling on a plan — and no wonder, considering what actually happened — so Pauline's frontal attack and the charge of Alzheimer's caught her completely off-guard. It was a really low blow, equivalent to treating her as if she were a demented old woman. Catherine told me later that she was beyond furious. Pauline has never played fair when she's wanted her way. Catherine says she immediately jumped up and ran from the kitchen into the main salon, with Pauline in hot pursuit. She tried to lock the door behind her, but Pauline pushed forward and was again right up in her face. Catherine says she tried to calm Pauline down. What are you doing, are you mad? Stop shouting!

So, of course, Pauline started shouting even louder: You are shaming our family. My children will not be able to hold their heads up. Catherine tried to counter with: But you were the one who introduced us, you *like* Tim, you are always telling me how much you like him. She says that Pauline actually smacked herself on the head — as in a cartoon — and wailed, Oh, if I had only known!

Then Pauline screamed that our relationship was incest! Pauline, I am not his mother, what are you talking about? Catherine countered. But you are *old enough* to be his mother. What you are doing is completely immoral, Pauline screamed back. Catherine tried to tell her that we are planning to marry but have not consummated the relationship, and will not until we are wed. Pauline said, Well then, you are just *stupide*.

Then, switching gears yet again, Pauline began screaming that Catherine had been overtaken by the Devil, that she had been seized by a sexual demon. The Devil has come into our house in the form of Tim. Pauline continued to wail that the château would never be the same. You have ruined it for me. Think of what our father would say. Is this a man he would have approved of? Then her final thrust of the sword: Catherine has caused her children to lose their faith in God. She was their sainted aunt, so pure, so perfect, and now look what she has done to them. Catherine said that their faith couldn't have been very deep if it was so easily destroyed. Then she left the room, shouting, I have had enough!

When I arrived at the château later in the day, entirely unaware of the storms inside, Martine-Marie, one of Pauline's granddaughters, saw me getting out of my car, and instead of greeting me excitedly as she usually does she ran like a scared rabbit into the house. Then when I entered the kitchen, the whole of Pauline's tribe shot up and scooted out of the room without a word to me. Uh-oh. Catherine quickly ran to me, and her eyes poured out her distress. Pointing back toward the salon, she said: Listen to that. Sure enough, every few seconds there was a loud banging noise. It's Pauline, she's just wandering from room to room, slamming doors. She's been at it for the last hour. Catherine said she would tell me later what had happened, but that it was better if I left now. There was no point trying to tame the beast in the heat of rage. She would come to see me the next day. Needless to say, I didn't want to leave, but ultimately I knew it was the best thing to do. I didn't have a very tranquil night; my brain was completely flooded, and I had to drink a half bottle of cognac before I finally fell asleep.

When Catherine came to the *mas* the next day, she looked so wounded and down. I had never seen her like this before. She was walking from her car, shaking her head and saying, Only your own sister could behave so barbarically to you. All my life, I have been amazed by the brutality that family members can inflict upon each other. They can get away with behavior a stranger could be put in jail for.

She is also very suspicious of how Pauline found out about us. How did she know? she kept saying. Who told her? She is certain that Yvette said nothing.

Given the violent scene at the château yesterday, I had been worrying all morning about the possibility of Catherine telling me that we must stop seeing each other. I was up at six, and I managed to hack all the brambles away from the sheep barn, something that ordinarily would have taken days (or, more accurately, would have been put off indefinitely).

We brought coffees into the garden, and Catherine quickly moved to speak first, saying that she would understand if I had second thoughts about continuing together. I, of course, had prepared my own speech, making the same offer. So our protestations of willingness to back out for the sake of the other rose to the level of grand opera, until we just got tired and decided we'd prefer a good meal and a glass of wine. Obviously, Pauline's intention was to throw a cluster bomb into the middle of our relationship with the hope that it would not withstand the opposition. Not so fast.

Love, Tim

Madame Pauline LeDuc to
Bishop Rabine, Diocese of Cahors

Dear Bishop Rabine,

Please forgive me for imposing on your valuable time, but I write to you about a matter that is most urgent to my family. You have been a special friend to the Benoir family over so many years, and we are eternally grateful to you for being such a comfort to our mother when she was dying.

I sincerely believe that my sister, Catherine, is in grave danger. Catherine is a woman of very noble character. When our mother became ill fifteen years ago, Catherine moved from Paris to Château de la Rive to take care of her full-time. She has always been giving to her family — my children and grandchildren regard her as their sainted aunt and are completely devoted to her. Although a very eligible woman, Catherine never seemed to want to get married and have children; in fact, I believed at one point that she would become a nun and enter a convent. That didn't transpire, but she has always been close to the Church.

Our mother died, as you know, six years ago, and since that time my poor sister has been too much alone in our family house through the winters. I tried to give her relief from the heavy burden of the care of our property, but of course I couldn't be there much of the time because of the needs of my very large family. Last year, I met a young

American artist who had bought a farm in a neighboring village and, hoping to relieve some of my sister's loneliness during the winter months, I impulsively asked my sister to invite him for lunch. My sister enjoys painting and I thought they would have much in common. The young man had a very charming façade and was amusing company, and over the ensuing months we took him into our house as a friend of the Benoir family.

But now we realize that he is a wolf in sheep's clothing. My sister is convinced that this American is in love with her — which is ludicrous, as she is twenty years older than he. This fiend has preyed on her vulnerability, and as decisive evidence of his complete lack of morality, all the while he was working his way into Catherine's heart, this instrument of the Devil was living in sin with another woman. And now, behind our backs, they have made plans to be married.

I am most worried for the well-being of my sister, as I think this man has designs on what he believes to be Catherine's substantial estate. He has completely betrayed his friendship with me, but I confess that I must blame in some part my own naiveté and lack of vigilance.

In my sister's defense, I know she would not knowingly put her family in such a difficult position, and I fear she is now extremely ill with Alzheimer's. For the past year, I have noticed many signs of this illness, but I admit shamefacedly that until now I had not faced up to the possible consequences.

I fear for the honor of my family and I pray to God every day to protect my sister from a terrible fate.

I have also written a letter to His Holiness, which I enclose and that I hope you will judge worthy enough to pass along to him. As you may remember, the delegation you led to Rome had such a memorable audience with him, and I still feel deeply his words to me personally.

With my respects to you, Monseigneur
Mme. Pauline LeDuc

Château de la Rive

Chère Yvette,

Oh, my dear sister, all your fears about Pauline's reaction to news about Tim and myself have turned out not only to be justified but even more horrible than either of us could have foreseen. When she arrived at the house without warning, she came right up to my face and screamed that I had Alzheimer's. When I see you, I will fill you in on her laundry list of accusations, but as you can imagine, it has been very upsetting. *Elle est très méchante* . . . like a horrible child.

Yesterday, I went back to see Père Fleury at the rectory. As I walked into the room, his eyes filled with fright as soon as he saw me, and he began shuffling backward — which is not the best thing to do, considering that wooden leg.

I had come to see him with my concerns about how to

deal with Pauline, but it was obvious that Pauline had already reached him to pour her poison into his ears. I asked him directly if Pauline had been to see him, and his face immediately became extremely pained and more prunish, if that's possible, and he began stammering his protests: she is very concerned about you, there is nothing I can do, forgive me, I cannot condone such a union, and on and on, pathetically. God must have decided to extend special protection to him on this day, as otherwise he should have expired right then and there from extreme moral cowardice.

If that were not enough, Josette told me that Pauline came unannounced to her house yesterday afternoon. Josette was sitting in her front room comforting a young neighbor who had just lost her mother, when Pauline, without any notice of the tearful young girl, burst in and began ranting at Josette that, as a pious woman of God and my friend, she must do everything she can to prevent this sinful relationship.

I am at a loss as to how to contain her, and I can only pray that once she is able to recognize that Tim and I are genuine in our feelings for each other, she will have no choice but to acquiesce. The best outcome I can imagine is that her gigantic emotional storm, with lots of lightning and thunder, will play itself out. Let us hope. But she is not one to get over anything easily, so we may be in for a long siege.

I am now more grateful than ever for your loving spirit.

Catherine

Mas La Viguerie

Dear Mom and Dad,

The way things are going at Château de la Rive, maybe Catherine and I should just fly to Las Vegas and be married by an Elvis justice of the peace.

But short of that, yesterday I went to see the mayor at the *pharmacie* to get information about the logistics of getting married in France. At first Catherine and I planned to see him together, but then we thought better of it, small-town politics and gossip being what they are.

As usual, the mayor and the boys were in the front room watching a soccer match on TV, and from their shouts it was obviously a very important game. The mayor winced when he saw me, realizing that he would have to drag himself away to talk to me. He motioned me back to the dusty stockroom, otherwise know as his chambers, and as I glanced back at the boys, you could smear their wry amusement on bread like jam. They will obviously have a lot to talk about at my expense for at least the next couple of weeks.

The mayor put on his official face, and I got a very thorough explanation about how marriage works in France.

Unlike the United States, where you can marry officially in a church or synagogue or wherever you choose, France recognizes only a civil marriage. When I looked surprised, he shrugged and said, *Voilà*, monsieur, one of the lasting effects of the French Revolution; separation of church and state was finally made official in 1902. Also, Catherine and I can't just marry anywhere we want; as a French citizen, Catherine must marry in the town hall of her official residence, which in her case can be either Cajarc or Paris. The "marriage banns," a relic of medieval times, must then be posted for ten days at the town hall. If the posting of banns passes without event, those still absolutely determined to pursue marriage (the mayor's sly words) must arrange a ceremony within three months. And then suddenly his attention fastened on the boys screaming at the TV, and he ran out of the room, calling back to say that as far as the rules governing a religious marriage, we should consult our local priest.

Please send me a copy of my birth certificate — it has to be notarized. Only one of the many documents I need. The French are truly document-crazy.

Your son, Tim

Mas La Viguerie

Dear Mom,

Having disappeared for over a week (thereby giving us a little breather), Pauline, armed with two daughters and the accompanying sons-in-law and their assorted children, arrived today at the château and claimed to be staying indefinitely.

Pauline clearly feels that their presence will have a powerfully persuasive effect on us. They moved into the "adjunct" château building this afternoon and remained there quietly through the night and the following morning — although there was one unfortunate incident. Martine-Marie ran out of the building to say hello to me as I was going into the kitchen, but was quickly pulled away by Solange, her mother. As she was dragged away, we heard her wailing, But why can't I say hello to Uncle Tim? Catherine was furious about the incident and wanted to go immediately to confront Pauline, but in this case I had the cooler head and convinced her to let it go.

In the afternoon of the next day, Pauline asked to speak to me privately. She was so warm in her approach that I thought she was going to say that she was sorry for all the problems, that she was just initially so shocked, but now she wanted to make peace. She asked me to follow her to the library at the far end of the ground floor of the château. As far as I knew, the only use of this room in the present day was by grandchildren playing hide-and-seek; I had glanced in the room only once, noticing the magnificent floor-to-ceiling fireplace, but the rest of the room was depressingly neglected.

Pauline led me by the hand to one of the two chairs facing the fireplace, then sat in the companion chair and pulled it in closer to me, as a warm fireside chat was clearly her intention in the staging of this intimate moment. *Quelle histoire, quelle histoire,* she kept saying over and over. Given that the fireplace had not been lit in at least fifty years, reality undercut Pauline's careful scene-setting. It turns out that Pauline sees herself as *ma protectrice*. She has decided to make my future sex life her personal concern. Tim, my dear, dear Tim, she kept repeating, you are a young, virile male. Perhaps now it is possible to imagine a life with my sister, who admittedly is still quite beautiful at her age, but, believe me, I understand more fully than you can possibly know "the life of a man." Pauline worries that I will abandon her poor sister, who is so vulnerable and whom she loves more than life itself. Tim, my dear, dear Tim, it may not happen right away, she said, sighing for effect, but inevitably you will find Catherine a repulsive old woman, and reject her and turn to others. It would be through no real fault of mine because as "a young, virile male," a phrase she kept repeating over and over throughout the conversation, I can't be expected to curtail my urges.

Instead of pushing in Pauline's face, which is what I really wanted to do, I let her ramble on and on while I turned my mind to the larger question of the seemingly extraordinary amount of attention paid in French culture to men satisfying their sexual needs. I found it really interesting that Pauline showed deep concern for my future happiness, while she doesn't seem to be remotely concerned with Catherine's. I suppose Pauline could argue that she wants to spare her sister the inevitable pain that would come from a relationship with me. I am a man, so of course I will reject Catherine, of course, of course, of course.

I tried to spare Catherine the worst of what Pauline had to say to me, but she was very quick in surmising the tenor of the conversation. She says that what has shocked her most about Pauline's whirlwind of opposition is that not only does it show how fixed and antiquated her ideas are, but also that Pauline really doesn't know her at all, that in fact she is just another stick figure in Pauline's ongoing life drama. Pauline got married very young (seventeen), and immediately after, she and her husband moved to a suburb of Paris, and the baby machine got to work, putting out one a year. During the time Pauline was having all those babies, she and Catherine did not see a lot of each other. Pauline therefore knew nothing of Catherine's life in Paris, little about her friends or interests. So the gap grew very wide.

Catherine believes that the most rare form of family affection is a real kinship of the mind. Like the truly self-absorbed and childishly tyrannical, Pauline has no sense of what her sister Catherine wants for herself. What I have to marvel at is that Pauline has absolutely no self-consciousness about her behavior. I suppose it is what we admire in tyrants. Genghis Khan had nothing on Pauline.

Stay tuned, Tim

280 West 73d Street, New York

Dear Tim,

If this were not happening to my own son, I would be completely fascinated by what your romance has stirred up, but I struggle with my own feelings about what you are doing. Not to put too fine a point on it, but in all the years I was imagining your future, this scenario would have been the last I could have come up with!

Let's be honest: you have not lived in France very long, certainly not long enough to peel back the layers upon layers of complexity in French society. You yourself have shown in your letters how aware you are of France's complicated continuous history over thousands of years, and now you are coming smack up against the collective unconscious of the French. Given the violence of the reaction you have received, I get the sense that your relationship with Catherine has activated a whole trunkful of French taboos.

Taboo number 1: older woman with younger man. Old French goats can carry on all they want with very young women, but not the other way around. I've written several essays on Colette, as you know, and taught classes on her writings. Her famous story *Chéri,* about a beautiful, rich courtesan past her prime and her much younger lover, emphasized as it unfolded how ultimately repugnant many see the relationship between an older woman and a younger man. There are deep misogynistic veins running through French culture.

Then there is the French attitude toward outsiders. I hesitate to use the word *xenophobia*, but you can't discount the French need to remain purely French, which requires keeping anything *not French* at bay. Everything is hunky-dory until you presume to cross over into their sacred territory, and anyone who comes from the "outside" is at a terrible disadvantage. And Americans are a special case: the ultimate love-hate relationship. When I lived in France, I was rarely introduced as Marjorie. I was always Marjorie — pause — that charming American girl.

Then there is the French idea of marriage. Your father says that individual happiness, in the sense that Americans understand it, is not a value in France. For the French, the emphasis is on the family/tribe. When Pauline said that your relationship with Catherine ruined the château for her, it was not as bizarre from a French point of view as it might sound to an American. Marriage is for the continuation of the paternal line and benefits the family, period. Any expectation on your part that consideration be given to your and Catherine's love for each other is laughable from this point of view.

And why do the French have so much disdain for the puritanical sexual ideas of Americans? It follows from the above. Marriage is a social contract — love need not enter into it at all — so finding love outside the marriage can be almost a necessity for protecting the contract. Remember when Mitterrand died? Both his wife and his mistress were at his funeral. Try to imagine that happening in the United States. And remember the troubadours? The underlying point of those stories of chivalry was that romantic love could exist only outside marriage. The deep and true France is not far from a feudal society.

And between sisters, let's never forget the problem of jealousy, and the powerful need of siblings to spoil each other's happiness. From this distance, it appears that sister Pauline can't stand the fact that there has been a power shift. Until now, she has been controlling all the pieces on the chessboard, dominant in terms of her position not only as the only married one, but as the family broodmare who has produced nine children. What I think she probably fears most is your influence over Catherine. Catherine, if she marries you, will no longer be a controllable piece on Pauline's board. Which of course is not to excuse Mme. LeDuc's extraordinary behavior.

I hope you don't think I'm just piling on. But I needed to put all this down on paper, as much for myself as for you. I think you should realize what you are up against, and perhaps it will help to see that in the deepest sense it is not personal.

Your Mom

Mas La Viguerie

Dear Mom,

Mom, you're the best. I have to say that at first I found
your letter hard to absorb all at once — and I suppose I
did think you were piling on — but now I've read it over
several times and there's no question that you're right:
I've managed to hit the mother lode of taboos. What has
stayed with me most from your letter is the idea of needing to spoil someone else's happiness. Frankly, I don't
want to spend more than two seconds on the possibility
that Pauline's jealousy toward Catherine is sexual, but I
have a feeling that Freud would have had a field day with
this woman.

I'm coming to grips with how lethal such a jealousy
can be. A notice was posted on my door summoning
me to court in Cahors to show my papers. They claimed
it was just a routine immigration check, but I doubt it.
Nothing terrible happened; I was just made to wait for
hours and then a gendarme summoned me into an office,
scowled at my documents, then sent me to another office,
where yet another functionary scowled at them. It's a good
thing I crossed over to Monaco for a day when I was in
St.-Tropez so that my passport was newly stamped.

Then yesterday, a "labor official" showed up. He asked
about the work being done on my property, claiming
someone had reported that I was using "illegals." I did
hire two men a few weeks ago to help me do some work

151

on the studio. I want to get it in reasonable shape so I can work here comfortably during the day and not have to go to the studio at the château. I don't have a clue if the men I hired were actually illegals, or even what this means in France.

Catherine has become alarmed by these occurrences and she thinks that Pauline is actively working to get me deported. I had a hard time believing this at first, still suffering under the illusion that this woman "likes me." But now Catherine and I agree that we must go ahead with the marriage as soon as possible. A benefit I hadn't originally planned on is that I will then automatically have dual citizenship. We've decided not to go Cajarc for the civil ceremony, but to Paris, where there is less chance of interference from her family. Catherine believes that Pauline can't wield quite the same power in Paris as she does here.

Pauline's husband, Pierre, by the way, who has stayed very much behind the scenes, showed up at the château one day. Mostly, he leaves all the dirty work to his wife. He asked to speak to Catherine and sat her down for what she later called a "university lecture" from Professeur LeDuc. First he listed her responsibilities to the family. Then he gave her an extended profile of my motives and underlying psychological makeup — clearly I have a deep mother complex and am a very disturbed individual. As for Catherine, he pities her, aging as she is and trying to pretend to be young again. She was completely appalled by what he had to say to her, what she described as low-grade sociology, pigeonholing and labeling, treating her like a specimen.

So my image of pastoral French life has been completely turned on its head. Even Chicken Lady has been acting strangely lately. She has not been by the *mas* in weeks, and now when I pass her house in the mornings she is not out in the yard with the chickens but inside watching a brand-new television. The chicks look very neglected. I can only think that a relative died recently, because where did she get the money for the television?

To add even more drama, when I got home this evening there was M. Bête hovering around on the road. He has been doing this for the last week. He goes through with the sheep and then stands around for a long time exuding a preternatural stillness. The sheep stand still as well. Thank God I took down the stone wall on Catherine's advice, so at least on this issue there is calm. I hope he's not working himself up to another major battle, as I have enough on my plate right now.

Tim

Mas La Viguerie

Dear Mom and Dad,

Very early Friday morning, Catherine and I set off for Paris under "cover of darkness." We borrowed a car from a friend of Josette's, leaving Catherine's car at the château and my *deux-chevaux* at my place, so as to throw the vigilantes off our scent. Don't laugh: Catherine is convinced that Pauline has been using neighbors to feed her information about us — hence the elaborate getaway plan. In Paris, we plan to post the banns for our marriage at the town hall of the Seventh Arrondissement, Catherine's official residence. We are also scheduled for a medical exam (I can't wait for this), after which we submit all our documents and get our marriage license. As expected, the French document fetish is keeping us busy.

Luckily, we have our own spies in this cloak-and-dagger game. Josette is solidly in our corner and, as pure and saintly as she is, she has an enthusiastic political side. Given her status as someone whom the Virgin blessed with special attention, she has very cozy relations with many members of the Church hierarchy, and last week she got wind of a letter Pauline wrote to the bishop of Cahors. I of course find the idea of writing to a bishop otherworldly, but Josette, with a twinkle in her eye, said that I shouldn't worry — after all, little is done quickly in the Catholic world, and Catherine and I would probably both be in the afterlife before anyone got around to our situation. She then said that gossip, on the other hand, travels like lightning, and she is confident that she will soon find out the content of Pauline's letter. More and more, I'm getting to love this woman.

A few days before we left, I wrote to Pauline to say that should Catherine and I marry I was renouncing any present or future claim to the Benoir estate. I included a document that Maître Lussac had drawn up, which, by the way, he thought was a completely ridiculous idea. Renounce possible claims to an estate? Voluntarily? What a dumb American.

But at least I'm on record as having no intention of interfering with their family business, and maybe I can blunt any escalating financial paranoia on Pauline's part. I also included a delicately worded passage (that took me hours to compose) saying I wasn't about to take multiple mistresses, or embarrass Catherine in any way, and that I loved and respected her sister and promised to take care of her until the end of her days. Catherine had a big laugh over my convoluted prose and said that I didn't have the deep linguistic heritage of the French that would enable me to say what I wanted to say without actually saying it, nor did I have the duplicitous game-playing nature required for this writing task. She also said that my forthrightness is what she likes most about me, and it's what protects *me* in the long run, and what protects *her*, and then she said even more pointedly that when we're married this quality will protect us both. Much food for thought.

Anyway, once Catherine and I were on the road — without everyone's judgments swirling around us — we felt a wonderful release. Catherine began a game of discarding judgments out the window. There goes "Alzheimer's," she said, and I countered with, There goes "gigolo." Catherine: "cradle robber." Me: "poseur." Until we got ourselves laughing wildly and not thinking about all the negative garbage that has been thrown our way. Before getting to Paris, we decided to make a detour to Giverny, the village made famous by Monet. I particularly wanted to see the Museum of American Artists, which has a collection of paintings by Americans who formed an artist's colony there at the turn of the century. As we would discover, they produced credible work, heavily influenced by Monet, naturally. Catherine says it's well known that Monet originally welcomed the Americans, but then as their numbers grew larger and larger he felt oppressed by all the copycats and eventually shunned them completely.

We went to eat at the Hôtel Baudy, where most of the American artists used to live, and had a delicious warm duck salad, lemon tart, and a celebratory bottle of champagne to wash them down. As we sat reveling in our happiness, I got more than a little mushy, having ordered a second bottle of champagne, and began exclaiming to Catherine that she always seems as light as champagne. She thanked me for the compliment by saying it is a very French notion that a woman should always be *gaie*, with sparkle, wit, and charm. She feels we owe those close to us our best and most buoyant side — what is the point of unloading our heaviest thoughts on those we love? But then she said that we must also be serious when the events of life demand that of us. Otherwise, an inappropriate "lightness" can turn into a "faux finish," a dangerous and horrible fake. Ultimately, it is love that gives us the permission to be light because love takes away the pain of looking for love, or believing that love is lost to us forever. In my intoxicated state, I began thinking that these Frenchwomen are amazing. When they're good, they're not only very good, they're incredible, and really, really light, and I waved to the waiter for another bottle of champagne. But the practical, and suddenly much less light Catherine, said, No, no, my love, we'd better go now.

We arrived in Paris just as the sun was setting and, oh God, the city looked astonishing, washed with pale gold. The iron lanterns on the bridges over the Seine spilled their light onto the black water in shining streams. The traffic, however, was horrific, and the noise level was really scary, a whole different symphonic pitch from New York noise. After living in the country for the last two years, it was a blast of the reality of city living.

So I finally got to see the Benoir family's Paris apartment, which I have been hearing about all these months. It is two floors of a *hôtel particulier* in the rue de Varenne in the Seventh bought by Catherine's great-grandfather in the 1880s. The high walls hide the building from the street, and large, heavy carved wooden doors open directly onto a cobblestone courtyard. When the building was erected, the space was for carriages, and so the parking now is extremely tight for cars. The street has a deserted gloomy cast at night, as in this part of Paris partic-

ularly life is lived behind walls and gates, and many of the old, grand houses have been turned into embassies and government offices.

The downstairs foyer alone is as large as a West End Avenue apartment. Catherine's great-grandfather's wealth had grown immense in a period of great prosperity in France before the turn of the century, and in 1890 he moved the family from their grand apartment off the boulevard Haussmann in the Eighth Arrondissement to this even grander one in the Seventh. Catherine says her great-grandfather came to regret his decision; when they lived in the Eighth, he was on the top tier of the social ladder and revered for his intellectual accomplishments. In the Seventh, he was never quite accepted by the aristocratic inhabitants and he hated the snobbery of the so-called *beau monde*.

And, Mom, you will like this, the Benoir family actually knew Edith Wharton. Her apartment in Paris in the early 1900s was in a *hôtel particulier* at 53 rue de Varenne, diagonally across the street from the Benoir apartment. There is a famous Benoir family anecdote about a great-uncle of Catherine's who became extremely enamored of Edith. He had never married and thought he would remain a bachelor for life, but when he met Edith he insisted that he had finally found his soul mate. But the family deemed her absolutely unfit, as not only was she an American, *quelle horreur,* but she was — double *quelle horreur* — divorced and forty years old. What Edith thought of him, we will never know, nor will we know how this poor man dealt with his quashed feelings.

The most beautiful room in the apartment is the front salon. As I walked in from the landing, I was knocked out by the grandness of its proportions — almost square, with elaborate curved moldings that seem to melt into fourteen-foot-high ceilings, and the most stunning seven-foot-high *boiserie* on its walls. Yvette told me with family pride that the *boiserie* walls were painted when the apartment was built and have never been touched since. The lovely gray wood walls still look absolutely perfect, which speaks to the artist in me of the quality of the lead paint used, which may or may not have killed anyone over the years . . . but I digress.

Yvette lives here on her own, a solitary figure in the twilight of her family's history. The apartment is so large that she rents rooms to a Russian opera singer, Mme. Olga Rossoff, whose vocal exercises serve as our alarm clock every morning. The apartment is in much better condition than the château, although it is just as frozen in time. Except for Yvette and the Russian, the place is empty. Real *living,* as opposed to just caretaking, is absent.

I bunked in brother Louis's old bedroom, overlooking the rear garden, with floor-to-ceiling double doors and gorgeous heavy brass hardware that you find everywhere in France. What are called "French doors" in the United States are puny echoes of real French doors. I found the room extremely daunting at first, with its mahogany wainscoting and a rich dark green and gold patterned wallpaper above it, and of course the ubiquitous Louis-Louis commodes and chiffonniers.

The bed was a very masculine statement, a metal fourposter with a tapestry overhang, very Napoleonic campaign was my first take, and there's a lavish bathroom with a magnificent curved freestanding nineteenth-century copper tub in the middle, and a gorgeous porcelain sink, with ornate sconces above. I came to Paris wearing my most decent clothes, a sports jacket and brand-new pants, but when I took them off in this room, they looked like thin rags. I glanced over at a photograph of Louis, splendidly decked out in a black suit, silk tie with impressive diamond stickpin (whatever happened to those?), and the only thing I could do was laugh.

Having seen members of the Benoir family in the veriscope photos taken at the château, it is easy to imagine them all together in this house. Mme. Benoir in the salon sewing, M. Benoir in his study reading, a housekeeper dusting, then children returning noisily from school, loud laughter among relatives gathered for a holiday dinner. But a house that was once so full of family life is now just a museum of the past . . . which sets one musing first on the brevity of life . . . and then on the universal need to live life as if it will never end. How do human beings bear the inevitable losses in their lives?

When I consider the above, I get more outraged by

Pauline's behavior. How many more years does Catherine have on this earth? But Pauline wants to deny her whatever happiness she can have in the here and now.

It got me remembering an undergrad comparative religion class. The professor liked to tell a Buddhist story I've never forgotten: You hold a beautiful glass in your hand, you admire it, you drink from it, but then one day the glass has been put away on a shelf, and sometime later it begins to get dusty and, as time passes, more neglected. Then years later, a wind blows the glass off the shelf and it cracks into pieces. And so the moral of the story is: even while you are holding the beautiful glass in your hand, *the glass is already broken*.

To be continued tomorrow.

Tim

Rue de Varenne, Paris

Dear Mom,

It's about ten A.M. and I am writing this letter sitting in the garden of the Benoir apartment — where, miraculously, I've actually had over an hour of sunshine. The garden is timelessly beautiful, with climbing rosebushes covering all the walls, and elaborately carved stone benches. Yesterday, as Catherine and I were walking down the rue de Varenne, I happened to look over to my left and was stunned to see the most spectacularly beautiful building and grounds at number 77, just a few houses down.

That is the original Hôtel Biron, Catherine explained, smiling at my reaction, built by a M. Biron as a grand monument to himself. For all his striving — the locals at first tried to stop him from building there, considering him a *parvenu* — poor M. Biron was to live in his mansion for less than a year before he died. Later the property was taken over by the government and subsequently rooms were given to artists to work in. The most famous was Rodin; Rilke also lived there, at one time as Rodin's secretary. Fascinating stuff — and what a difference from funky artists' lofts in SoHo. Now it is the Rodin Museum, which explains its splendid condition. After finishing this letter, I plan to head right over.

Last night, Catherine and I went to a dinner party given by one of her good friends, Nadine Gourdet. They went to *lycée* together, and she is now a major antiques dealer. This get-together marked my first meeting with Catherine's Paris friends, and I knew that the inspection process would be exacting to say the least, but I steeled myself for it by doing a lot of deep breathing on our walk over. I was pretty proud of myself for even agreeing to go, actually, because at a different point in my life I would have ducked the whole thing.

We walked along the boulevard Raspail, crossing over from the Seventh into the Sixth to the rue du Cherche Midi, a long narrow street with chic restaurants and boutique hotels, which leads to the boulevard du Montparnasse. The nondescript doorway of Nadine's building promised nothing special, but once inside we stepped into a jewel box of an apartment, overlooking a lavish garden. The space was a little claustrophobic for me, what with so many objects meticulously presented, but I did feel that there was a sincere love of the beautiful. If not my cup of tea, I had to admire it.

Besides the chic Nadine, there was a journalist named Claude, very haggard-looking and smoking nonstop; a designer named Roger, very gay; and a very sophisticated Welsh terrier named Claudine. So I got a snapshot glimpse of Catherine's previous life through her friends. As usual at a dinner table in France, conversation revolved heavily around the food, but here in Paris the attention seemed to lean more to the *cachet* of what was being eaten rather than to its taste: Nadine had bought the cheese from the *best* cheese store in Paris, the delicious veal from the *best* butcher on the Left Bank. And all this was mixed in with lots of gossip, most of which I couldn't follow.

At a certain point, Claude the journalist began telling a story about his experience with his counterpart at the *New York Times*, which veered into the negative characteristics of Americans, and the even more negative characteristics of New Yorkers. I began tuning out, as it was just as bad as Americans talking about the French. Claude kept making apologetic nods to me, as if to say that when we talk about Americans we're not referring to you, of course. Catherine glanced over at me and smiled, and knew exactly what I was thinking.

After quite a bit of delicious champagne and a perfect prune tart, we moved away from the dining table to the front salon for coffee and brandy. Nadine then brought out an album of photographs, settled herself on a settee, and motioned for us to gather around. As she turned the pages of the album, she pointed out all the photographs of Catherine, saying over and over again: Look at her ravishing beauty, wasn't she stunning . . . And then Catherine's friends enthusiastically launched into stories about her life in Paris. Catherine was extremely embarrassed and kept waving at Nadine and the others to stop, but I have to say this was definitely my favorite part of the evening. I hadn't realized how much attention Catherine had received as a painter. There were lots of photos of her at her own gallery openings. And of course there were quite a few photos of her with Le Philosophe, giving the impression that they went *everywhere* and were known to *everyone*.

Are her friends disappointed in her less than celebrated choice of mate? Not only probably — without a doubt. But despite knowing this, and despite reservations about the guests, in retrospect I was surprised at how much I actually enjoyed myself at the dinner: so much high energy, such spicy conversation, such great food . . . but I certainly couldn't make it a steady diet.

The Paris diary *continue demain.*

Tim

Rue de Varenne, Paris

Dear Mom and Dad,

On Monday, Catherine and I walked the ten blocks to the town hall of the Seventh Arrondissement on the rue de Grenelle to deliver our documents. As is typical of my experiences in France, the first clerk we encountered was M. Nasty. Then just when we were thinking we were sunk and getting nowhere, M. Nice intervened. So the marriage banns have been posted, and after waiting the obligatory ten days, we will return to Paris for our civil ceremony, performed in this same town hall. It's not exactly a terrible hardship to have to return to Paris.

Later that day, we had a meeting, arranged by Yvette, with the new head priest at Ste.-Agnès La Vièrge, a small church in the Seventh where the Benoir family has attended mass since after the war. Catherine and Yvette's parents were married in this church, and it's apparently common practice to schedule the civil and religious marriage ceremonies back to back. I'm all for this.

Père Bosquet — extremely boyish and athletic-looking — greeted us at the door of the vestry, warmly shaking our hands. He has a quick, flashing smile, which would prove a little unnerving, as the smile didn't always appear when there was anything to smile about.

He asked me if I was interested in converting to Catholicism. I was expecting this question, though I wasn't sure how frank I should be with him. Spiritual questions have been on my mind a lot lately, but I am a long way from settling my mind in any way. I finally said that I knew it was not obligatory to convert in order to marry a Catholic in the Church, but that conversion was certainly something I would consider down the line and that if I were to convert I would take the matter very seriously, which would require study and might take months.

He seemed to agree that I should take as much time as necessary and then said that he would be happy to provide guidance when and if I was ready to convert.

He walked with us out of the church (he was going to take a jog in the park — The Jogging Priest!), then called out as he took off that as soon as we set the date for the wedding, we should let him know immediately.

We didn't head back to the Midi right away; we were in Paris, after all, so why not spend a few more days hitting museums, something we had never done together. I was particularly interested in going to the Carnavalet in the Marais to do some research for my murals. There are lots of eighteenth-century drawings and paintings of rural France in the collection there. What a feast for the eye and an amazing treasure trove it turned out to be. And going with Catherine was a special treat, as she knew exactly what was on every floor. She said she used to go at least once a week when she was living in Paris.

Sitting in the museum café later in the afternoon, we began batting around the idea of living in Paris. Certainly we could live more privately here, but Catherine said she could not go back to painting in Paris: too many parking tickets! She then explained that to paint outdoors in Paris meant driving somewhere, struggling to find parking, dragging around your easel, paints, and brushes, and then paying those stupid parking tickets. If nothing else, it was too expensive.

I'll write again when I'm back at the *mas*.

Love, Tim

Mme. Pauline LeDuc to Père Bosquet,
Ste.-Agnès La Vièrge, Paris

Dear Père Bosquet,

Thank you so much for contacting me so quickly after your interview with my sister and Tim Reinhart. God help us in this terrible time.

I am astonished that my sister would post the banns at the town hall and then go to our family church without discussing it with us. It is just more evidence of how much she is under the influence of this American and how completely he has separated her from us. Until now, my sister Catherine has always put her family first. She has been a saint to my children. That she and M. Reinhart would go to Paris for such a purpose and not let us know . . . I pray for her soul.

Believe me, *mon père,* you don't have to apologize for your inability to convince them that they should not marry.

My sister has a stubborn temperament — how often I have had to deal with it — and she always thinks she is right. And now, God help us, she is under the spell of this American. It's clear that the Devil has taken hold of my sister's soul, and it would be difficult for God himself to make her listen to reason.

My daughter Solange says that you have been so comforting to her during this difficult time. She and her husband are completely mortified by her aunt's behavior.

Our family has always supported Ste.-Agnès La Vièrge with our hearts and our resources. My father and mother were devoted to your predecessor, Père Gagnier, whom I also remember fondly, and each of my nine children has been baptized there. Thank you for all the new information about the wonderful work you are doing for a new chapel and the prospectus of financial needs. I have spoken to my husband so please be assured that we are prepared to make a generous donation.

May God bless you, *mon père,* for your support in these dark days.

Respectfully yours,
Mme. Pauline LeDuc

Mas La Viguerie

Dear Mom and Dad,

Here is the latest mind-boggling development.

We were home from Paris for four days when Catherine received a letter from the *procureur de la République* summoning us both to Paris for an interrogation at the Palais de Justice — on stationery so magisterially French that it was enough to give a person a heart attack. Receiving such a letter is essentially the equivalent of the attorney general of the United States writing you about your impending marriage.

Catherine was stunned. We were sitting in the château kitchen having lunch, when Bette brought in the mail. Catherine told her to just put it down, but Bette said, Madame, you must look at the mail now. Catherine stared hard at her and said, Don't wait around, I know you are spying for Mme. LeDuc, and you should immediately consider other employment. But Bette was defiant: You cannot fire me, she said, whipped around, and left.

So we had to go back to Paris immediately. This time we didn't drive, but went the next day by taxi to Cajarc and then took the local train from Cajarc to Cahors, where we picked up the fast TGV train, which got us into the Gare Montparnasse in the early evening.

We went right from the train station to meet Le Philosophe. His name, by the way, is Bertrand Denys . . . oddly enough, the first time I actually heard his name said out loud was when Catherine began talking about him on the train ride. Catherine says she had resisted contacting him at first, but then realized that she couldn't think of anyone else who was more connected on all levels of government.

Notwithstanding Catherine's assurances, I was apprehensive about meeting Denys, worried that I would come off as a massive idiot . . . or even worse, someone that only a Frenchman with a language suited for it could lacerate perfectly. So I said: Maybe you should meet him on your own, and of course Catherine saw through this, and said, No, no, no, it will be fine, this isn't just about me, it concerns us both, and, besides, you have every reason to be confident in yourself. Denys is not any more special than you, he certainly isn't smarter from what I know about you both; he is just a product of his culture and someone who knows how to play his part perfectly. This is one of the things I like most about Catherine, her simple presentation of a situation, analytical and warm at the same time. And she definitely had me. I really couldn't weasel out. So, okay, maybe I'd appear to be a massive idiot, but at least not a coward as well.

We met Denys that evening at the Brasserie Lipp on the boulevard St.-Germain, where apparently he has a standing table whenever he's in town. I found this meeting place quite ironic, as when I was in Paris during my sophomore college break, a group of us tried to get into this famous brasserie, as we had heard it was where all the giant literary and political luminaries had hung out — Proust, Camus, Hemingway writing his WWII war correspondence, de Gaulle, Chirac in the present day. So these cocky Harvard guys arrived to take their place among them. The maitre d' spotted us before we even got through the front door and blocked our entrance. He actually told us that there wouldn't be a table for us no matter how long we waited.

When Catherine and I walked into the front dining room, Denys was reading a newspaper at his table, positioned diagonally across from the front entrance, giving him instant visibility to anyone entering the restaurant. His back was against the wall — like a Mafioso, I couldn't help thinking. I guess it was still early for dinner at this restaurant, as there were just a smattering of people dining, but there were at least a half-dozen waiters standing around, keeping their eyes discreetly trained on Denys's table. Denys quickly rose as soon as we came toward him, kissing Catherine on both cheeks and then shaking my hand vigorously.

And so we sat ourselves down. Bertrand — he asked me to call him that — ordered his standing dinner of *choucroute,* the Alsatian house specialty — and I decided I would try it as well. The waiter bowed and scraped shamelessly, treating Bertrand like royalty, which in some way I guess he is in France. Only in France would a "philosopher" have this kind of status. The *choucroute,* by the way, was delicious, but a pretty heavy meal to eat regularly, so you have to wonder about Bertrand's cholesterol count.

Throughout the dinner, Bertrand was extremely polite to me, although there always was a hint of amusement under anything he said to me directly (but maybe he has a permanent twinkle in his eye?). Then Bertrand began to address the matter at hand; he seemed to speak in whole paragraphs, as if he had already written a newspaper column on the story of our romance and his crucial part in it — two thousand words in *Le Matin?* — and was now simply reciting from the copy. From what I could pull out of the lush web of words, he had made a few phone calls very discreetly and believed that he had been able to do some good work on our behalf, but time would tell. He ended with a few modest flourishes. *On verra, on verra.*

As we walked back to the rue de Varenne after dinner, Catherine talked about her years with Bertrand, beginning in the late sixties. Denys had become famous at a very young age for his writings — about the philosophical implications of communism — and was extremely compelling, she said. And in a man's world, a woman necessarily gets her education and sophistication from the men who choose her. Denys was the first man who took me seriously, she said. *Chérie,* you have a very good brain, were his words. As a child, she had a voracious appetite for knowledge, but was kept isolated by her parents and the ingrained habits of their class. Her mother was talented and rich in imagination — and so much fun to be with — up until Catherine was about twelve they had a marvelous time together. But when she got to age thirteen, they began to have many conflicts. Her mother wanted the best for her, but in practice that meant that she wanted to control how Catherine participated in the world. Both her father and mother wanted to restrict whom she could know, what she could read, where she could go . . . they kept insisting that they were fostering her proper education. But for Catherine it became a prison. Whenever Catherine and I talk about such things, I get an impromptu lesson in the many layers of French society.

The next morning, I went out myself at dawn for a long jog. It was only drizzling, but I geared up with a Gore-Tex jacket for the inevitable nasty weather on its way, and I hit the pavement with a lot of energy. The rue de Varenne is even more forbidding in the early morning hours, with not even street cleaners to animate its lifelessness.

I set out without an overall plan for the jog, knowing that, hey, I was in Paris and I could always find my way back. After a mostly sleepless night, I hoped that at the end of the run I would have sorted through recent conflicting thoughts. There are times when I think, What am I doing? Am I just playing a part — you know, a heroic figure caught in the web of a family drama — by Racine, maybe? Let's face it, up until now the perceived needs of my ego have always driven me forward. Now I'm caught up by events I don't have any control over. In all my previous relationships with women, I was always fiercely protective of my separateness and individuality, so "going with the flow" or "surrendering" to a relationship doesn't come naturally to me. But is this the great paradox of love? That we get needs met by surrendering and meeting the needs of the one we love? Every day I'm bowled over by what has happened to me.

When I got back to the rue de Varenne, about eleven A.M., I was tired from at least ten miles of jogging and at least a million mental miles of overintellectualizing. But most importantly, I was starving. Catherine was sitting in the kitchen with Yvette, coffee and croissants on the table, and they were laughing and having the best time. Yvette, who is always singing, had apparently decided to sing the "Saga of Catherine and Tim" as if it were a Gregorian chant, so she and Catherine were chanting back and forth to each other when I walked in, and I quickly picked up the song myself, at which point Catherine whipped around, and her face lit up with joy.

And you know what? I forgot about any stupid heavy stuff and decided to forget rowing backward on the rapids and just go with the goddamn flow.

After lunch on the same day, Catherine and I set out for our appointment at the Palais de Justice. There was still no letup in the weather; it wasn't raining exactly, but the sky was slate gray and extremely threatening. This day would turn out to be the most surreal experience in our marriage quest, and that's really saying something. The Palais de Justice buildings, with their magnificent conical roofs, extend for seemingly endless blocks along the Seine on the Île de la Cité. Look over there, Catherine said. That is called the Conciergerie. It's where Marie Antoinette was held in prison. Do you think our sin is as great as hers? What medieval tortures do you think are awaiting us? Usually Catherine and I find things simultaneously funny — but not in this case.

After following a clerk down an immensely wide corridor with black striped marble floors and vaulted ceilings, we were shown into a plain bureaucratic cave with nasty lighting. The procureur assigned to our case turned out to be a thin, platinum blond woman, about forty-five, in an austere salt-and-pepper suit, with a red pin perfectly placed on a lapel. Yikes. Severe in the way only a Frenchwoman can be severe. Madame motioned to me to sit in a chair in front of her and asked Catherine to wait outside. In the stillness, I could actually see dust floating through the cramped space. Madame didn't waste any time on small talk. Are you aware of the allegations against you, monsieur?

This threw me. The mayor had mentioned to me that it was possible, given our ages, that some investigation might be made into whether Catherine and I were entering *un mariage blanc,* the delicate French way of describing "a marriage in name only." But he assured me that in most cases it was just a formality. *Il faut le subir,* he said.

But allegations? What allegations? My mind raced through the various events of the past months. Could it actually be possible that my fight with M. Bête could prevent me from marrying? At this point, Madame took a letter out of a folder and began to read from it in a loud declamatory voice. My fogging brain picked up that I was a fiend who had misled the poor susceptible Catherine, who was probably suffering from Alzheimer's, and not only did I claim to be a Catholic, I also claimed to be deeply religious, further deceiving Catherine. The letter was obviously from Pauline, or someone in her family, but Madame refused to tell me the name of the sender.

I tried to say that the accusations were completely ridiculous and weren't even worth answering, but Madame lifted her shoulders sharply, as if to indicate that she was offended for all of France. I got the distinct impression that she thought that this American had one hell of a nerve getting involved with a Frenchwoman, who did I think I was, and why didn't I just get on a plane back to that stupid America now.

I wasn't very good in my own defense, but I don't think what I actually said mattered much, as Madame clearly was determined to play the scold. Then she brusquely announced that she was finished with her questions for me and asked me to wait outside so that she could talk to Catherine.

I sat alone in the hallway on a stone bench for what seemed like forever. At one point, I bummed a cigarette off a passing woman lawyer. I had spotted her long before she reached me, briskly walking, *clickety-clack,* in her high heels on the marble floors, tight shiny pants under her black robes, with the standard white rectangular judicial neckpiece. She lit my cigarette, and I impulsively asked her why it was that I'd come across so many women in the legal profession. Have the men all left? Oh no, she said, they are very much there, but more *en haut*. Women do all the "kitchen work," she said and laughed, then continued *clickety-clacking* down the hallway, swinging her briefcase and dragging on her cigarette.

The procureur's office door finally opened and Catherine and Madame came walking out together. I don't know what I expected, but they seemed to be talking like old girlfriends, their heads very close together. Catherine was murmuring something, then Madame Procureur murmured something back, and then Catherine said something else, and this continued until they kissed each other on both cheeks, and then Madame straightened her hair, gave Catherine a quick wave, and closed the door behind her.

As we walked down the hall, our footsteps echoing (yes, I'm building up the drama here), a small smile came onto Catherine's face and she said: we have permission to be married. I let out a shout that resounded in the vaulted space, turning quite a few heads down the hallway. Catherine said that she explained to Madame Procureur the complex dynamics of her family life — you know how sisters can be with each other, she told her — describing the ongoing problems over control of the family estate and Pauline's various power plays, and Catherine could see that something, she wasn't sure exactly what, was registering with this woman personally. But ultimately, she said, it came down to saying that she had thought long and hard about all the ramifications of a marriage to me and that she was determined to proceed.

Did she think that Bertrand Denys had used his influence? I asked. Since we'd met I had turned him into something of a punching bag, and I wondered if I was being fair. Catherine said that maybe he had helped us, but his name never came up and so we will never know. Her energy shot up dramatically and she said: What difference does it make anyway?

Then Catherine kissed me and clapped her hands and said that now we deserve a delicious meal! I offered to take her to the best restaurant in Paris, big sport that I am, but she said, No, no, no, too fussy, too formal, and in any case she much prefers bistro cooking to "designer" food. At first I thought she was worrying over my money, but she said absolutely not, she hadn't been to a four-star gourmet palace in years, she didn't enjoy them anymore, because after all it's more about them than about you. So we went to a small bistro near the quai Alexandre III, where Catherine knows the owner and his wife, M. and Mme. Jacob, both big and robust, with identical ruddy cheeks and round bellies. She introduced me to them as her fiancé, and for the first time when there were other people around we both felt entirely comfortable with this idea. We looked at each other, reading the simultaneous thought, and laughed.

Madame bear-hugged Catherine, then me — nearly lifting me off the ground and cracking my back expertly in the bargain — and Monsieur rushed excitedly into the kitchen to make us something very special. First came oysters, superfresh and ice-cold, with a ginger sauce, then a creamy sorrel soup, then a veal roast, then a *mâche* salad, then cheese, then a cherry tart. I'm still not up to snuff on wine selection, but I know that the dessert wine was the famous Château d'Yquem. The meal was *exquis,* as Catherine said over and over, and here is where the French can knock you out with their loving attention and pride in food. Everyone was happy!

Love,
Tim

Rue de Varenne, Paris

Dear Mom and Dad,

Our actual wedding day turned out to be very rushed and strange. We felt we had to get the civil ceremony performed right away — before Pauline could put another disruptive plan into motion — so we went first thing to the town hall and after haggling with M. Nasty and M. Nice, we managed to squeeze in our ceremony for three P.M. that day. It was — *naturellement* — yet another one of those foul, damp, gray Paris December days, just the right mood for a wedding!

Catherine called Père Bosquet at Ste.-Agnès about arranging the religious ceremony, but he claimed he was not given enough notice and in any case he was going out of town. Catherine was distressed by his cool attitude, but we had no time to worry about it. So we put the religious ceremony on hold until we were back in the Midi. At least we have gotten the civil ceremony under our belt.

The ceremony at the town hall took less than twenty minutes. Yvette, who has been amazing through this whole process, was there as a witness, and at the very end of the ceremony, standing in the back, to my surprise, was Le Philosophe.

The mayor and various officials worked themselves into a state of excitement when they saw Denys, further evidence of his celebrity. Later I asked Catherine what she thought about his showing up. Had she told him the ceremony was today? She didn't know how he'd found out. Her guess was that he came out of either real *sentiment* or just *amusement,* or maybe a combination of the two. And the problem is, we will never know what it was that compelled him. Then her eyes took on a glint as she said, And neither will he! It will be all about him in the end in any case. *Tant pis.* And then she laughed and kissed me.

After the ceremony, we all got soaked in a heavy downpour. When we got home, we gathered in the grand salon with the concierge from next door, several neighbors, I never got their names . . . and Catherine's friends Nadine and Roger, who apologized for Claude the journalist, who was on assignment. We all sat down in a ring of chairs with dust covers. A more motley group is hard to imagine.

Yvette, poor soul, had been thrown into a complete tizzy over organizing a little reception for us. Catherine tried to talk her out of it, but she was adamant. Catherine says that of the three sisters, Yvette is the one with absolutely no domestic abilities. The three girls were essentially raised as eighteenth-century Jane Austen heroines. They sang, painted, played the piano, but were not expected to take care of a house or earn a living. Catherine eventually came to love to cook and garden; Pauline is a great organizer; but Yvette is completely without household skills of any kind. First she fretted about what to serve, as she probably until this moment had never planned a menu of any kind. So finally she went to her local café, where she takes most of her meals, to consult about getting some food delivered. Catherine was sure that we would get *steak-frites*, but that was fine with her. Yvette spent the morning trying to find platters to put the food on, laughing at herself for not having looked into the cupboards in years. She finally called a housecleaner to come in and help her wash some dishes.

Then Yvette announced that Olga, the Russian opera singer–tenant, had been pressed into service to provide music for the reception. The woman was going to sing Yvette's favorite Puccini aria, *"O mio babbino caro,"* in which our heroine implores her father to let her marry the man she loves. (An interesting choice, don't you think?) Anyway, Yvette kept saying, Oh, how she wished Maria Callas could do the honors, but she hoped Olga would do a reasonable job. Catherine looked skeptical but said nothing. One of the things I really like about her is her cool equanimity. She is willing to let things take their course.

As our little group sat waiting, Yvette kept assuring us that the musical part of the reception would begin at any moment, but in the background we could hear Olga on the phone loudly berating her accompanist-boyfriend for not arriving in time. Then Olga slammed the phone down and said that the man was a complete idiot, he doesn't like to travel when it rains, and then she absolutely refused to sing. I must have my accompanist!

To top it off, Yvette forgot to pick up some champagne, which we definitely needed to take the edge off things, so I rushed out to buy a few bottles.

When I got back with the champagne, dusk was setting. As I walked in the front salon, our group was sitting so quietly that I got the strange sensation that I was looking at a reception party of ghosts . . . ghosts in a twilight of life in the rue de Varenne, and at any moment they would all turn to dust. And just when I was thinking that this was one crazy reception, the salon took on a beautiful glow, the present neglect buried by the evening light. I turned on all the lamps, at least those with bulbs that worked, and Catherine found some candles.

Without any warning, Olga began softly singing a Russian folk song a cappella. A famous wedding song, she told us later. As the verses began, she sang in a whisper, and then she slowly increased her volume and intensity, and in that magical way of Russian singing the sound became so intoxicating that we all began to sing along without knowing the words. Then Olga repeated the opening verse again, and we sang round after round. The room turned darker, so the outlines of the architecture seen through the windows faded, and it was as if we were transported to a wedding in the sky.

Tim

Catherine's diary

The Catherine who used to write in this diary no longer exists. The Catherine who writes tonight has a brand-new heart.

But except for what I share with Tim, my happiness must remain my private affair. My friends say they are happy for me, but I know that they think my being with Tim is beneath my station.

Unfortunately, they would much prefer my being unhappy to being inappropriate. But I don't care at all what others think. I know I have something that is better than just good . . . it is pure gold. With the grace of God, I know the difference between a love-filled state and an empty one, and I who have been asleep for so many years feel complete gratitude for it.

Nadine has been married three times, bless her, and it always starts happy, happy, happy . . . but then not long after, she begins complaining that the man is a complete beast to her. So she goes back to her little Welsh terrier for comfort, and is soon on the hunt again.

Although Yvette has been perfect to me, there are many things I cannot tell her. She is pure, she is wonderful, but she still carries that terrible wound. I will always remember how our father, who was extremely exacting when it came to suitors for his daughters, spoiled Yvette's chance to marry that lovely fellow, Jacob, who sang like a God and adored her — but was, God help us, Jewish — by putting those punishing roadblocks in her way. I know she struggled for several years with her fear of defying him. And just when she had worked up her courage, poor Jacob died suddenly in a car accident. Then sadly, I think Yvette closed that portion of her heart for good.

From the moment Tim and I entered the bedroom after the wedding reception, I don't remember a second of unease with each other. The physical part of our love flows as easily as the mental. The lovely hours went by before we even thought about being hungry or thirsty, and I particularly loved our going down to the kitchen after midnight to bring up water and fruit, which we immediately devoured.

It's not just the incredible gift of physical love at a time in my life when I thought I had to give up any dream of it, but also the gift of a "sweet love," a love without tyranny, from either his side or mine.

I am even grateful for my years alone after Maman died. I grew stronger in myself and came to know I could survive as a woman alone. There was a kind of cleansing, a taking away of my youthful "neediness," which pollutes relationships when we are young.

With Bertrand, there was always the back-and-forth of my saying: I love you! But you don't love me! Then I would pull away, then he would pull me back. So much gamesmanship over dominance and submission, mostly on his side (dangling other women in front of me), but also on mine. For if one side is playing games, then the other plays games back. But with Tim, I never stop to think, Does he really love me? He has a rare inner confidence. I doubt he would choose to see himself this way, but it shows in the fact that he is not at all insecure around me or threatened in any way and has no interest in game playing. Bertrand radiated self-confidence, but there was always that need to swagger around to affirm his masculinity.

There is really a lot to be said about trust building gradually, without the distraction of extreme passion. Mme. de M. took care of the illegitimate children Louis XIV had with his mistress Mme. de Montespan — for whom he had a great sexual passion but little trust. Louis's trust of Mme. de M. came gradually, particularly from noticing how she took care of his children. He once said that she was a woman who knew how to love and that he thought it would be very pleasant to be loved by her.

They were great everyday companions, they spent hours each day just talking to each other, and those who think she was without any femininity or sexuality underestimate her . . . and ultimately cannot explain why Louis needed to marry her and why this previously randy old goat remained faithful to her for the entirety of their marriage. After Louis died, Mme. de M. wrote to a friend that she had given up cosmetics and perfume, saying that she had lost him for whose pleasure she previously had used them. Obviously her revelation speaks volumes about how much she wanted to please him, and not just with her mind!

My biggest struggle has been to control my rage at Pauline's invasion of my privacy. It is all I can do to keep myself from strangling her. I have never experienced such rage before. She actually sees herself as God, ordering life according to her commands. I can understand disapproval, but obstruction and active interference are something else again. Real evil can be generated when, like infants, we see ourselves as the center of the universe. Mme. de M. said that even a little happiness attracts a great number of enemies.

Josette says that I must restrain myself from retaliating. Wounding Pauline back merely draws me into a terrible battle, for which there is no end. She says the need to control comes out of fear and jealousy and that I must try to forgive Pauline. My anger is like nothing I have experienced before, but I know that Josette is right.

I do wonder sometimes, Am I living in a complete fantasy? Am I a madwoman overtaken by a sexual demon, as Pauline would like me to think? And will I soon wake up and find that Tim has disappeared? But in truth, I really have no such fears. There is an inner *knowing* . . . a coming home.

Mas La Viguerie

Dear Mom and Dad,

We are two weeks back from Paris, and Catherine and I are now married in the eyes of the state, but not in the eyes of Mme. Pauline LeDuc.

Catherine and I had mistakenly believed that once we were officially married, Pauline and her troops would resign themselves, but on the contrary, they have become even fiercer in their opposition.

Pauline announced to us in the château kitchen that she is completely disdainful of our civil marriage. She claims that the only marriage the family has recognized, since long before the French Revolution, is a religious marriage. Their father would be appalled; their mother would be appalled; and the whole family is hanging their head in shame.

She then said with shock in her voice that Catherine

has been seen staying overnight at my place — and yes, it's true, Catherine has stayed over here several evenings recently. At first, I was worried about how she would adapt to the Spartan accommodations, given what she is used to, but because of her deep knowledge of this part of the world and her feeling for its unique nature she concentrates on everything positive and beautiful here and doesn't concern herself with discomfort of any kind.

So we are really enjoying ourselves, but according to Pauline we are *living in sin,* and under God's eyes our re lationship is essentially incest. You can't have children! she shouted. Marriage is for having children! Catherine told Pauline to stop talking nonsense and that she was very angry with her for sending that ridiculous letter of denunciation, but Pauline was unrepentant. Yvette says that Pauline genuinely cannot understand a marriage such as ours. Marriage for her is utilitarian, a function of society. Marriage as a spiritual union, or a companionship of the like-minded, is beyond her ken. It is hopeless to get her to understand.

So it's no wonder that the reality of being married has not sunk in yet. At first I did not understand why it was so necessary to get married in the Church right away and, legally, the civil marriage is all we need. But now I realize that until we go through with a religious ceremony, Pauline will not stop her relentless attack.

Catherine has been trying to contact Père Bosquet in Paris for days without any success. She thinks Pauline has gotten to him — just as she had with Père Fleury — and that he is dodging the call. So much for a young priest being more helpful to us.

And we wonder how Pauline knows exactly when Catherine is staying at my place. I now seriously suspect that Chicken Lady has been spying for Pauline. One afternoon, soon after Catherine arrived at the *mas*, I saw Chicken Lady hurrying away — which would explain the brand-new television set!

Catherine and Yvette prevailed on their father's brother to come from Paris to the château for a meeting to help them work out new living and financial arrangements. After much stalling, Pauline had no choice but to consent to this meeting. Catherine has been very concerned about Yvette, as through no fault of her own she has been dragged into the battle. But in her quiet, catlike way, Yvette is very shrewd and knows how to protect her own interests. Catherine says that Yvette has a unique ability to avoid Pauline's attempts at direct confrontation, a case of the cat always being able to elude the bulldog.

I was leaving the château just at the moment that the uncle and his wife pulled into the circular drive in a black Peugeot. Catherine's father died in the late seventies, and when it came time to settle her mother's estate, his brother was the one who handled all the negotiations.

Uncle Paul-Henri is a sturdily built and serious figure befitting his stature as an important government scientist. Catherine quickly moved to introduce us as he got out of his car, and he shook my hand vigorously. As a couple, the Paul-Henri Benoirs look very country; both wore nearly identical tweed suits, and the wife was without makeup or adornment. Catherine says that they are embarrassed by Pauline's behavior, and she hopes that her uncle can provide a reasoned voice. She says that he has worked out a plan for how to sell the château and divide the assets if the sisters cannot come to terms on sharing its use in their lifetime. But Catherine feels selling the château is too extreme a measure, and she herself has been working on a plan for dividing its use, giving Pauline plenty of time there on her own. Catherine and I can divide our time between the château and my place, at least temporarily.

As prearranged, I went back to the château late in the afternoon to pick up Catherine and drive back to the *mas*. When I got there, Uncle Paul-Henri and his wife were just leaving, and again, they were extremely gracious in that special French warm-cool style, he shaking my hand vigorously, she shaking her head eagerly.

As Catherine and I drove back to the *mas*, it was hard to ignore that in a region that can have spectacularly beautiful nights, this night was outdoing itself. But Catherine, usually so responsive to every nuance of weather and sky, was scarily silent. It was pretty clear that the meeting didn't go well.

Finally Catherine began to laugh in the way a person laughs when it's the only thing left to do. I was just about to begin my carefully prepared speech, she said, when Pauline just blurted out that I should relinquish my share of the château. Just like that. And then Pauline folded her arms across her chest.

Uncle Paul-Henri — perhaps used to more civilized meetings in his professional world — tried to say, Pauline, let's try to be reasonable and let everyone have her say. But Pauline cut him off with: Catherine can have Tante Marie's cottage for her lifetime, after which it goes back to my children.

Until now, Pauline has refused to let anything be done to the cottage, allowing it to deteriorate — at the same time claiming she loved it beyond reason — and now she generously offers it to Catherine. Poor Uncle was at a loss. There was little more to say, and Yvette just went back into the kitchen to get yet another piece of chocolate.

Catherine says a long period of silence held them at the table, none of them able to look at the others. Pauline then jumped up and claimed she had to go to Paris.

Uncle suddenly looked twenty years older and awkwardly said that he didn't want to keep his wife waiting any longer. And then Catherine and Yvette just sat together finishing the box of chocolates, as it was now stunningly clear to both of them that underlying Pauline's histrionics about our marriage is a ploy to gain control of the château, that Pauline is using the fact of our marriage as a wedge to force Catherine out.

After hearing about all this unbelievable maneuvering,

I was so guilt-ridden that I had to pull over by the side of the road and stop the car. You can't live like this, I told Catherine. Maybe they're right; I am a selfish bastard and have brought nothing but trouble into your life. I worked myself up into a serious fit of remorse.

Catherine thought that I was being ridiculous. Even if we hadn't married, she said, the problems of the château and the Benoir family dissolution were ongoing and inevitable. Don't give yourself so much credit, she said. Yes, it's true, our marriage initiated a crisis, but a crisis brings the possibility for change. It brings to a head like a terrible boil (not a lovely example, she said and laughed) what has until now been a complete stalemate. No decisions could be made, and the château was slowly sinking. Now Pauline has shown her hand, her intention of marginalizing her sisters and then taking over all the property for her own family. So Catherine said she actually had some hope that at least now there will be some kind of forward movement. So please, you cannot feel guilty, she told me and went on in this vein until I finally calmed down and we continued to the *mas*.

Just as we got to my place, who was coming out of the door to my kitchen but Count Fishy! Without any embarrassment for having entered my house uninvited, he was full of bluster and good cheer. It's about time you arrived, he proclaimed. I've been here over an hour waiting. He obviously had been raiding the refrigerator, as he was munching on a piece of *saucisson*.

You will be very pleased to know, he continued, that I have found the underground passage used by the Maquis. Come this way. So we dutifully followed him to the sheep barn and, sure enough, when he moved back some big timbers at the far wall, there was a space we could actually walk into. It led into a natural cave, which he told us one could then supposedly walk through and come out to the road. After about five minutes of walking stooped over and wondering if there was no end to it, we suddenly came out into daylight on a field and saw that about fifty feet in front of us was the *crèche* on the side of the road! Because of the deceptive angle of a configuration of rocks, if you stand on the road looking past the *crèche* toward the rocks, you do not see the cave opening.

Count Fishy waved off what he seemed to view as our silly enthusiasm, and then he told us a not very happy story. One night, members of the Maquis left the *mas* and went through the passage on their way to bomb a bridge — the one I think I showed you the commemorative plaque of when you were visiting. The first Maquis members to get through the underground passage were able to blow up the bridge, but the last few coming through were spotted and killed right there by the *crèche,* and that apparently was the end of my *mas* as a hideout.

The count was getting into his old battered Citroën when he pulled from the front seat something wrapped in newspaper. He first proffered it with elaborate politeness to Catherine, but then quickly began to unwrap it himself. It was a large porcelain tureen with lavish gilt detail, and it looked very valuable. In honor of your wedding, he said, unsuccessfully trying to bow at the waist, hindered by his massive belly.

I was amazed at this generous gift and shook the count's hand vigorously in thanks. He kept protesting, It's nothing really, and then he quickly got going before we could thank him further. I was surprised that Catherine didn't try to thank him, as it was not like her.

Later, as we sat having a coffee, she finally came around to saying something: You know, I had heard rumors that the count had been a member of the Resistance. It seemed so unlikely at the time and I never took it seriously, but now I believe it to be true. I was completely floored. This pudgy old royalist? In the Maquis? But Catherine pointed out that the Midi region resisted the German occupation more than any other region in France, and both the highborn and lowborn played their parts in the Resistance, including her father — and remember, the war was nearly sixty years ago, and Count Fishy was a vigorous young man then.

Just as I was about to say that people are full of extraordinary contradictions, Catherine pointed to the tureen, now sitting majestically on my paltry pine table: It's quite beautiful, isn't it, really magnificent. I was mystified by her strange tone. Finally she said: It went missing from the château many years ago. My mother was quite distressed at the time, as it had been a wedding gift from *her* mother.

And then Catherine said that whether it was actually a "gift" or just a "returned item," it is much appreciated, she really *must* send the Count a thank-you note.

And then we both began to laugh and kept laughing and laughing and didn't stop until coughing fits took over.

Through it all, laughter is what keeps us sane.

Tim

P.S. I am off to L'Abbaye Curemonte for about two weeks to begin work on my murals.

L'Abbaye de Curemonte

Dear Catherine,

I got here just as the sun was setting, and as I biked up the main drive to the abbey, I thought I was arriving in a beautiful ghost town. There had been a shower a few hours earlier and the lawns were glistening, very magical, but also disconcerting, as if I had set out in the morning in this century and arrived later that day in the fifteenth.

I'm so glad you suggested that I ride my bike up here. If I had just driven up in my car, I would have taken in very little around me on the way. Being so close to the ground on a bike, I was able to enjoy subliminally the shifts in scale of the landscape, and the unique colorations of the Limousin seeped into my brain. So as an extra bonus, I got some wonderful ideas about how to approach the murals. The Limousin is beautiful, with its gently rolling hills and lush green meadows, but it's way too tame for my taste. I definitely prefer the fierce bleakness of the Lot. I made a short stop in Fresseline, the town where Monet painted his famous *Study of Rocks,* which I read somewhere got $25 million recently at auction. I made a halfhearted attempt to find the actual rocks he painted, but then I decided to forget it, remembering all those Monet imitators, and as much as I admire Monet I want to rely on my own eyes.

My benefactor, Frère Bénédict, the one so impressed with my landscapes, spotted me as I was parking in a visitor's space and then escorted me to my room. It overlooks a gorgeous garden and is definitely monastic, about seven feet by nine, with white walls, a narrow bed with a cross above it, a dresser, and a small desk.

The next morning I went with Frère Bénédict to see the gallery room, and the instant we walked in I had a massive anxiety attack. No one had mentioned that it was a rotunda! In all my imaginings of the room over the last weeks, I always saw it as a rectangular room with entrances at two ends and murals on the two facing walls. In fact, there are four separate entrances — a quite stunning design — but trying to anticipate the sightlines as one enters the room presents brutally complex perspective problems. And the size of the panels necessary, at least twelve of them, is way beyond my expectations.

I told Frère Bénédict that I had to rush back to my room . . . Not used to their kind of breakfast, I called back to him ... And as I fled I kept trying to think of the French word for "the runs." Really pathetic. When I got to my room, I instantly wanted to get down on my knees and pray. It seemed the only thing to do! But somehow I managed to calm myself, and then slowly, slowly, over the course of the day, I began working up some ideas on paper. The next morning I began digging around in the monastery library, where I found some amazing drawings from the nineteenth century done by a resident monk, and many other treasures. So I began to feel more confident, and now I think I can conquer the perspective problems and actually have some fun. It will probably take me about two weeks, maybe a few days less, to do the preliminary plotting.

Used to working quickly, I found myself whizzing around in an environment where all others were moving decidedly slower. I would put the pedal to the metal on the way to the gallery room, and not a few times I found myself rushing past monks coming the other way and almost knocking them down. Then I realized that these monks may walk slowly, but that doesn't mean they are out of touch. I noticed several of them walking around with earpieces attached to their cell phones.

At night, I've come back to tackling Pascal's wager. Needless to say, my interest in the spiritual has accelerated for pretty obvious reasons, not the least of which is being here. Pascal began his analysis by saying, God is or God is not. There is a higher intelligence, or there is not.

And in the absence of certainty, it makes more sense to believe than to not.

A lot of bozo amateur philosophers (in case you didn't know, *bozo* is American slang for *idiot*) have claimed to disprove his wager, for a lot of dumb reasons . . . like, God wouldn't want people to make bets. In graduate school I remember feeling a special envy toward Einstein, and I'm not talking just about his genius, but about the fact that Einstein, being Einstein, could say whatever he wanted and so much of his personal writing contains his own brand of spirituality. The atmosphere at Harvard when I was there was decidedly antispiritual and didn't allow for such musings. It was a brash macho world and really "smart guys" didn't go around thinking about whether God existed. No doubt, they didn't like the competition!

But in fact spirituality and mathematics go hand in hand, as the more you work at it, the more you become aware of how vast the universe is and the more humble you become before it. Even Stephen Hawking said that the mind of God is the ultimate undiscovered mechanism.

To experience love is to experience something that is beyond logic and can't be quantified. What accounts for the fact that you are a presence in my mind at all times, that I don't feel at all separate from you? Can an equation be made for it? Ultimately, it is wholly *experiential;* that is to say, it *is* because I experience it. And once I experience it, it opens my mind to what is beyond rational understanding.

I worry about you at the château, but at the same time I know you can take care of yourself. Pauline, being a fantasist, has no idea how strong you are. Next time I need to come up here for an extended work session, I hope we can come up together, as you say you've never been to the Limousin, and we'll have lots of fun exploring together.

All my love,

Tim

P.S. I completely forgot to mention a surreal experience I had this morning. I was walking down yet another corridor, and suddenly an American voice called out, Tim, what are you doing here? The voice turned out to belong to Billy Bucknell, someone I went to school with in New York.

After I got over the initial shock of his being at the abbey, we went and had a coffee in the dining room. As we talked I realized his presence here was not really that strange. His family are very upper-crust New York Catholics; his mother is a socialite who runs the equivalent of a French salon, and retreats to French abbeys is what they do a lot. I did get the distinct feeling that Billy's stay was not entirely voluntary, that he had been sent to get him out of some kind of trouble. He can be wickedly amusing, and we immediately slipped back into New York banter. We had quite a few laughs about where the world takes you.

Even more love, T.

Château de la Rive

Dearest Tim,

Such an interesting story about meeting your New York friend at the abbey. It made me realize how much I look forward to traveling to New York with you.

Earlier this evening, I made dinner for my nephew Roger and, poor boy, he is mortified by his mother's behavior toward us. I kept telling him that he must not think that what has happened has anything to do with him, and so far he has managed to avoid any conversation about it with Pauline — although being Pauline, she has been pursuing him. When he began saying (as he poured yet another glass of wine) that he was determined to confront her and tell her what he thought about what she was doing, I got really alarmed and pleaded with him not to. Nothing would be gained, I kept saying. I can only hope he listens.

After he left, I sat for a long time trying to imagine what life was like for you growing up in New York City. I began to realize that because I have never been there and know so little about how life is lived there — or for that matter, in the whole of the United States — I couldn't possibly form a real picture of your school life. If you were French, I would know that if you went to this *lycée,* you were of this class; if you lived in this *quartier* of Paris, it said that about you; and so on. Yes, I would form a distinct picture of a French you; but on the other hand, my ideas would be cluttered with prejudices and class rigidities and would be distorted by them.

As I got into bed, I thought, Oh, what a beautiful gift I have been given in you. When I was a young girl, I was never allowed to socialize outside a small number of girls and boys that had been preselected by my mother. But now you and I can float above terrible stereotypes — you as an American male from a more open society, me as the product of a French class system that provided a depth of culture, but had a stranglehold on individual will. So I relish learning everything about you and look forward with joy to our continuing dialogue. I feel sure we will always talk openly, as the deep underlying trust between us will keep us from ever getting surprised or distressed by details of the other's life.

So as much as I am missing you here, I feel as you do, that you are completely here with me and that our "superglue," as you call it, is stronger than ever.

In fact, I've been so much calmer this last week that I have begun to work again. I went to Maman's studio yesterday to look at all the unfinished canvases I had stored there — quite a shock to see how many were piled up against the wall.

I can't really explain how it came to me, but somehow I was sitting sketching on a canvas, and my mind suddenly felt unhinged from my past methodology, and I began thinking of creating a "moving life." But this "moving life" would paradoxically still be in the form of a "still life." I don't know where this idea came from — merging two opposites concepts — but I got very excited by it, so excited that after hours of work I lost complete track of time. It was dark when I got up to stretch my aching muscles, and as I was pacing the room I suddenly noticed your Gorge de Limogne painting leaning against the wall. I could not take my eyes off it. In my heightened state of awareness, I saw so many things in it that I hadn't noticed before.

When you get home, I will tell you more about my reactions to this painting at length, but I think it has tremendous potential. I remembered that the last time you mentioned it, you claimed to hate it and threatened to burn it. Please don't be hasty. I think it is "gorge"-ous.

Some not so pleasant news: I am now absolutely positive that Pauline has corrupted Père Bosquet. I called him in Paris yet again this morning — finally getting him directly on the phone — and I could hear the fear in his voice, and then he claimed he had to rush somewhere and would call back. In confirmation, Yvette says that when she was at mass recently at Ste -Agnès, she saw two of Pauline's daughters coming out of his vestry wiping tears from their eyes, and there was Père Bosquet with his arms around them, comforting them. So we must forget about weak and silly Père Bosquet. As an American would say, Let's move on. We cannot help but find someone to marry us, as the miraculous Josette is on our side.

All my love,
Catherine

L'Abbaye de Curemonte

Dear Catherine,

Let me tell you the good news first. For the last three days, I have been working really well. In the mornings before beginning, I hike for at least an hour a day, just soaking up the local scenery, which helps to sharpen my thinking. There is a lot of wonderful Romanesque architecture here, which I'm very partial to, and quite a few castles dating to the twelfth century.

I have finally come up with an overall plan of attack for the murals. I'm going to make quick cartoon sketches for each panel, with a scale of one inch to one foot, which I can then work from when I'm back in my own studio. Now that I'm on top of a concrete solution, I'm very excited.

Once I got over my initial feelings of dislocation — where am I? what am I doing here? etc. — I settled down and began to get the benefit of the pace, and now I've come to appreciate the austerity of the environment, as it has allowed me to concentrate completely on my work. But don't get the idea that I want to be a monk!

Now the not so good news. Late this afternoon I was napping in my room after a really intense work session, when Frère Bénédict came to get me, saying that Père Abbé would like to speak with me. I was a bit surprised, as I didn't really expect to get to see the head man while I was here. The walk to his quarters seemed like miles, and

I tried to stop my mind from racing over the many ways he could tell me I was fired. Père Abbé's chambers were surprisingly small and homey, with comfortable worn chairs. Even in his monk's robes, he looked more like a prosperous local businessman than a monk.

He very graciously rose when I entered and motioned me over to a chair next to his desk. He held out a letter to me, saying that he had debated about whether to show it to me, but in the end he felt it would be better that I knew about it. His face showed no expression.

The letter was to him from Pauline. Along with it, she had attached my letter to her (relinquishing any claim to the château, etc.) and a report based on this letter from an "objective" handwriting analyst, as she referred to him. The analyst had concluded that, first and foremost, I had a gigantic mother complex, was also dangerously unstable, perhaps even homicidal, and almost certainly homosexual. Needless to say, sitting in front of Père Abbé as I read through the letters was violently embarrassing, more than horrible. I must have turned multiple shades of purple.

When I could manage to croak out some words, I finally said, Père Abbé, I can explain, but he immediately waved me off, shaking his head insistently. This is your private business. Clearly there is some stress in your life. Then after a long silence between us, he said that he hoped that being here at the abbey has provided a peaceful haven during personal difficulty. I couldn't think of a thing to say. Then after another really long silence between us, he asked how the murals were going.

So I managed to pull myself together to the extent that my mouth began moving, and I said that I was doing a lot of research on the landscape of the Limousin and had begun making preliminary sketches, at the same time working to get a sense of the whole, of how the individual murals would mesh together in a rotunda space. And how do you go about that? he asked after another long silence. So I told him about some techniques I'm working with, and I could see that he was genuinely interested. Keep up the good work, he said, and that was that.

Afterward, I had to go for a long bike ride to cool myself down. How did Pauline find out I was here? And her idea of sending the handwriting analysis? Truly diabolical. My first instinct was not to tell you about it, but then I knew I couldn't and shouldn't hold back anything from you. But please don't waste time getting upset or angry. I have already wiped it out of my mind and I'm back to work with a vengeance. Remember, pain is inevitable; suffering is not.

Expect me on Tuesday. I can't wait.

Love, Tim

Château de la Rive

Dearest Tim,

What an absolute nightmare experience for you. I'm

sure that Bette must have overheard one of our conversations and told Pauline that you were going to Curemonte. Otherwise I can't imagine how Pauline could have known that you were there. That I cannot fire Bette is completely infuriating!

Pauline's attempt to humiliate you is outrageous, but from what I can sense from Père Abbé's response, she is now overreaching and in this case made a complete fool of herself. She may be diabolical, but she is also obtuse and clumsy. Every day she becomes more and more of a silly cartoon character in my mind.

I would be much more upset about this incident, but I have some good news: I have found a priest to marry us! Père Pasquier is from a parish called Les Trois Collines, and when he called yesterday he said that he had heard about our situation and was willing to perform the ceremony for us. Though he claims to have called me on his own, I have a strong feeling that Josette has something to do with it. I count the seconds to your return.

All my love,
Catherine

Mas La Viguerie

Dear Mom and Dad,

I'm back at the *mas,* after two weeks at the Abbaye Curemonte. The work on the murals turned out to be a monumental sweat, and I panicked about once a day over the size of the project, but now I feel I have it under control. I managed to convince the powers that be that I can create individual panels in my studio, which can then be affixed to the walls but which will look like authentic frescoes. This method will allow me to work at home and much, much faster, as I won't have to wait until I can make yet another trip to the abbey in order to continue to paint. These monks are modern enough to understand that they can't expect me, or anyone else for that matter, to be sequestered there for the two or more years it will take to do the work, painting frescoes like a latter-day Giotto. They've moved a little since the Renaissance after all.

Anyway, more about this later. I'll send you some photos of the work in progress. Meanwhile, on the marriage front, it looks like there may not be a priest in all of France willing to marry us. I'm not exaggerating.

After Pauline scared away Père Bosquet, the priest in Paris, Catherine began searching for someone locally. Given the large volume of small churches in these parts, she felt confident of finding someone. Pauline's tentacles can't reach everywhere! Out of the blue, a priest from a small parish about fifty miles from here called and offered to perform the ceremony, and so we thought the issue was settled. But then, two days ago he backed out without giving a reason. This was ominous; something was up.

So yesterday we went to consult with Josette, our expert

on all matters ecclesiastic, meeting again at the terrific little café in St.-Pierre-Célé for lunch. The subject of this meeting made me uncomfortable, but the meal at the café is always a draw. Again there were only two choices on the menu, *blanquette de veau* or *tripe à la mode de Caen*. Catherine and Josette eagerly chose the *tripe* — so rare to find these days, they claimed, and then loved it extravagantly — but I still have some food resistance left, at least to pig's stomach, and went with the veal.

Josette filled us in on what she has been able to do on our behalf. She is certain that the priest from Les Trois Collines withdrew from performing the marriage on order of the bishop of his diocese, which is Cahors. This is the same bishop whom Pauline wrote to about our marriage. Apparently a marriage between a Catholic and a non-Catholic must be approved by the bishop of the diocese, so her guess was that Père Pasquier contacted him about performing our ceremony and the bishop nixed it.

Now here is where the tale gets even more convoluted. There has been gossip around that Pauline actually wrote a letter to the Pope trying to stop our marriage! Josette says that Pauline would have had to pass a letter to the Pope through the bishop of Cahors, who would then have to approve delivery of the letter. Josette isn't certain that the bishop actually passed the letter along, and she says it's highly unlikely that we'll ever know, as you don't go around questioning a bishop.

I asked Josette if she was putting herself at risk by

snooping. She gave me her most tolerant smile and said she never worried about such things, and I realized that my question was idiotic and went back to my veal, which by the way was excellent.

I found it unfathomable that Pauline would actually write to the Pope about us, but both Catherine and Josette were not really surprised by it. Catherine says I have to understand her family's deep Catholic ties with bishops, archbishops, cardinals. It's just a matter of writing to the boss. When I listen to all this stuff, it doesn't seem at all real to me, as if what I'm hearing is coming from a parallel universe.

After lunch, Catherine wanted to stop at the Virgin's church in the town square. She is very attached to this little church. It became particularly important to her after her mother's death. She felt terribly cut off and alone and got seriously ill herself. She says her body broke down from the years of stress. Denys became resentful. Her physical troubles became an inconvenience to him and he even went so far as to accuse her of having her own agenda and fabricating an illness to manipulate him.

She says he was not someone who could share a life. It was *his* life, and she was allowed only to play a part in it. At the beginning of their relationship, this was understandable. He had a "big" life. He was already very famous when they met, but as she began to mature and have artistic desires of her own, there was no adjustment in the dynamics of their partnership. She tried to find ways to continue, but there was never a merging, as she called it, and then suddenly she became "old" to him. It was a terrible time, a long dying over too many years, but she came to know that nothing lasts, not for men, not for women, but men, she said, laughing, seem to have a much better time of it until the end! So she began coming to this church over several years, and little by little her health began to revive, and finally she was able to cut her tie with Denys.

We sat in the first pew, close up to the statue of the Virgin, and my mind began wandering all over the place. As I was happily figuring out a particularly complex perspective problem, I had a most astounding sensation: The Virgin had given me to Catherine. I am a gift from her to Catherine.

I can't say that I actually heard a "voice," but I experienced the sensation *as if* a voice had spoken to me. Very, very strange. Although I would ordinarily tell Catherine about something like this, I didn't in this case. Catherine noticed my strange grin, but I just kissed her and we continued on home.

Knowing you, Mom, I'm sure you'll think I've completely lost my mind.

Love,
Tim

280 West 73d Street, New York

Dear Tim,

I am way beyond thinking you have lost your mind. The stories coming from you are taking on a surreal quality. I've had to detach myself from constant worry over threats, spying, ecclesiastical intrigue, financial finagling . . .

I don't want to embarrass you completely, but do you remember that your favorite boyhood book was *The Little Prince*? And do you also remember that in a momentary decorating fit, I had a painter draw freehand on the wall my favorite quotation from the book: *Voici mon secret. Il est très simple: on ne voit bien qu'avec le coeur. L'essentiel est invisible pour les yeux.* Amazing no, how fitting it is for you now? I'm actually sorry we painted it out when you were in your teens, but you said you didn't want any reminders of supposedly kiddie stuff.

For a wedding present for you and Catherine, we agonized for weeks, and then thought we would send you money to build onto your house, making it more comfortable for the two of you, should you choose to live there. But my ultimate present is staying on the sidelines and not meddling. Of course, this promise is easy to make, as there probably isn't a way to meddle even if I wanted to. Where would I begin?

Love,
Mom

Park Slope, Brooklyn

Dear Bro,

Here's something for you in the stranger-than-fiction category. Yesterday, I'm in the café at the Metropolitan Museum, having met my friend Alix for a little lunch and a little gazing at beautiful things, treating myself to an increasingly rare grown-up cultural activity. And who do we meet up with, but Billy Bucknell, and who is he having lunch with but your ex-girlfriend Kristen.

Although we were on our way out, they insisted that we sit down and have coffee with them. I really didn't want to, but Alix had already pulled up a chair before I could react, showing her true colors as a crass social climber.

I knew of course about Kristen's stay at your farm, and I *was* curious to hear what she had to say. So I just listened as she talked on and on, at first saying how *wonderful* this was and how *wonderful* that was, and slowly moving on to how primitive this was, how primitive that was, and finally to how she couldn't understand how you could possibly live there.

All the while Billy was fixed on my face, soaking up my reaction. Then he chimes in — like the cat that ate the canary — that he had also recently seen you, having run into you at a famous abbey in France. When I was understandably startled, he just loved it.

Since Billy's only religion, as far as I know, is gossip, anyone would wonder what he was doing at an abbey. He

213

was only too happy to explain how his über-Catholic family (his words) shipped him there. All the details of his story were, in fact, completely humiliating to him: his monster drug use, his cheerful embezzling from family accounts, how his family found out . . . a story that would be scintillating only to seventeen-year-olds — so I can only surmise that seventeen is still his real age.

Needless to say, these smug jerks got on my nerves, big-time. I never understood your attraction to Kristen. Well, of course I did, but good God, was she always such a witch? And after listening to Billy, I kept wondering why you told him anything at all about Catherine: that was walking right into the jaws of the ultimate gossip rottweiler. I pulled Alix from her chair, and we were out of there.

When I got home, I was feeling extremely dislocated. All my coordinates, as you might say, were off. Brad is away on a business trip, due back tomorrow, and our nanny was watching over a sleeping Tara. She actually refused to let me in the room for fear I would wake her. Can you believe that? We two are in a real power struggle, but that's a whole separate saga.

So in this emotional state, I got into bed hours early, an incredible rarity, and I found myself thinking back to old conversations. Remember when I was reading that book for a sociology class about "frames"? You really helped me understand that stuff, and I demolished the course. What I began remembering was how the social structures in which people interact subliminally govern behavior. But the more I thought about it, the more I began to worry, are you and I slowly moving outside each other's frames?

Holly

Mas La Viguerie

Holly, Holly, you are giving those two ultimately lost souls too much power. I can't believe I was dumb enough to say anything to Billy about my life here, but Billy Bucknell was always a weasel, and weasels are always out of frame. They don't count when you're trying to parse reality.

Even if I came back to live in New York, what would Billy Bucknell have to do with me? Absolutely nothing. I hadn't seen him in over ten years until I ran into him at the abbey. I'm happy to be out of his frame, but actually I was never in his frame to begin with. Think of it this way: social frames are fixed for those operating within them — like picture frames — but true feeling stretches far beyond the confines of any single frame. Mom recently reminded me of a Saint-Exupéry quotation that she had scrolled on my bedroom wall, but she probably won't remember the more important Rilke quotation I had over my desk: "Do not be bewildered by the surfaces; in the depths, all becomes law."

Love,
Your devoted brother

The Abbot of Curemonte to
the Bishop of Cahors

Dear Bishop Rabine,

I write you about the question of a marriage in the Church for Catherine Benoir and Tim Reinhart.

I recently received a letter from Mme. Pauline LeDuc, the sister of Catherine Benoir, expressing her opposition to such a marriage. She mentioned in her letter her correspondence with you about this matter. Mme. LeDuc certainly presents a very passionate argument against the union from her point of view. Not without some reason, she feels that her sincere devotion to the Church and her strong ties on all levels of the Church hierarchy provide additional persuasion to her arguments.

I made my own discreet inquiries about Catherine Benoir and have been assured by a good and faithful source that she is an excellent woman, perfectly healthy and retaining all her mental faculties. Tim Reinhart, the American in question, has just begun working at our abbey on murals for our new gallery room. He is a very talented and serious artist, and he has been working with great concentration on this ambitious project.

To get right to the point, my old and dear friend: Someone has to marry these people! They are both adults, they are vaccinated, and they are now married in the eyes of the state. Neither of them has ever been divorced, so there is no legitimate impediment to proceeding with a religious marriage. Surely we have enough to occupy us without becoming entangled in this essentially benign affair. What I sense is going on, behind the scenes, so to speak, could become an embarrassment to us. Here is a situation where we can demonstrate without consequence our compassion and common sense and show that we are not still living in the Dark Ages.

The final decision is of course yours, my dear friend, but I sincerely hope that we can handle the matter with discretion. As bishop of Cahors, you have jurisdiction over the priests who can perform the ceremony for them.

Respectfully yours,
Dom Antoine Constant

Mas La Viguerie

Dear Mom and Dad,

Thanks for the magnificent present. But most of all, thanks for your support.

I just found out that it was Chicken Lady who went to the Labor Department to denounce me for using foreign laborers, so I guess she's not in love with me anymore! We are now certain that she is watching my house and reporting back to Pauline. In addition, over the last week, the phone rings, and there is only breathing and then the caller hangs up. A few days ago in the mail, I received an actual death threat, just like in the movies, the individual letters cut from a newspaper and pasted. So it's fair to say

that I am feeling under siege. One night I went a little nuts and tried to convince Catherine that we should go to Italy and get married in a church there, but she feels strongly that we cannot let her idiotic family intimidate us; we can't let them think we take them at all seriously. She is very strong, and says she understands that as an American it is hard for me to know that Pauline's opposition will run its course and ultimately will not prevail. Most of the time I see her point. Then in the midst of some seriously disturbing stuff, something truly amazing can happen.

Remember I said that M. Bête had been hanging around the *mas* lately, just standing silently in the road with his sheep? Well, yesterday he appeared again, but this time he shouted out, Monsieur, come with me. A scary request, let me tell you, but for some unknown reason I felt safe to follow him, and I was really curious.

He led me to his property, the sheep clumping along behind us. It is only a quarter of a mile from mine but so different in mood. Maybe it's the austere white *causses* visible in the distance that make it seem singularly remote; and to add to the eeriness, the wind started whipping up wildly. Inside the yard was an extraordinary jumble of ironwork — literally hundreds of tangled iron pieces, old tractors, old gates, and old miscellaneous God-knows-what.

To my surprise, there was a handsome and substantial-looking two-story farmhouse, which now looked abandoned. I glanced in one of the windows and saw sheets over the furniture and large armoires standing around gathering dust.

I followed him into a large stone barn, and from what I could see M. Bête lives here by himself in a small section of it. I saw a narrow iron bed, which looked as if it's never made, just rearranged every night; a cast-iron stove; and, incongruously, a new shiny white refrigerator. On a desk made out of an old door were piles of ledgers and stacks of yellowing bills, and on the floor next to his chair an enormous pile of walnut shells, clearly his favorite snack.

After M. Bête picked up a key from his desk, we went around to the back of the barn to his underground cellar. On the way, I noticed a large copper vat in a nearby stone shed, which I took to be his distillery. I felt strangely honored to be going into his cellar, as I had heard that there's not a person in the area that has ever seen what he keeps down there. M. Bête turned on a bare ceiling bulb, revealing hundreds of dusty bottles in cases against the dirt walls. There were also about a half-dozen large wooden barrels, the contents of which emitted strange gurgling sounds. *Fermentation,* M. Bête said. Fortunately I had heard that in the process of making *eau de vie,* ripened plums are put into barrels and bubble unnervingly when they ferment — otherwise I would have been sure I was in the lab of Dr. Frankenstein and doomed.

M. Bête pulled a bottle from the racks, making a halfhearted attempt to blow off the layers of dust, then swiped two small glasses on his not remotely clean shirt. Then he poured out two hefty amounts in each glass and handed one to me. He was muttering to himself, *"Imbécile, imbécile,"* and I wasn't sure at all that he wasn't referring to me. He knocked back his own drink in one quick shot, but I resisted following suit. Just a sip of this stuff can strip the lining off the inside of your mouth. But I did go ahead and drink up. My throat closed for a few seconds, but I survived. M. Bête pulled another dusty *eau de vie* bottle from the racks and, bowing slightly, handed it to me and said, *Pour vous et votre femme.* It took several moments for me to realize that he was congratulating me on my marriage!

Then he wiped his hands on his pants and brought out a well-worn photograph from his shirt pocket. *Ma femme,* he said, and I swear his craggy old black eyes started to tear up. *Elle est morte.* He kept staring at the photo. *Il y a vingt ans . . .* And there was such grace in the way he held his wife's image in his massive battered mitts.

Catherine was just arriving when I got back to the *mas.* Although I was really eager to tell her about my unbelievable experience with M. Bête, I forced myself to save the story until we sat down for dinner. She had brought an armload of foodstuff from the château, beets, tomatoes, cucumbers, fresh eggs, melon, plums, figs, and several bottles of château wine. As she was moving about the kitchen, telling me about the latest wacko event back at the château, I could see that she was valiantly trying to tamp down the agitation invading her movements, which are usually so graceful. We are never at a loss for things to talk about, but for the last few weeks we have both been aware that we have been slipping into moaning about the high price we are paying for what we feel for each other. I hate to say it, but a tinge of victimhood has crept in. Clearly Pauline's campaign has been taking its toll.

It wasn't until we were having dessert (the plums were delicious) that I got around to describing what had happened with M. Bête. During my admittedly overexcited presentation, Catherine listened very patiently, but I was gesturing so heatedly that I knocked over the plate of plums and they flew and splattered all over the floor.

When I described how M. Bête showed me the photograph of his wife, Catherine gasped slightly and grabbed the edge of the table. I waited for her reaction. But in fact we didn't need to say a word to each other.

We both knew that M. Bête had given us an extraordinary gift. Anytime we fell into thinking about how difficult it was to be together, we had only to think of M. Bête and his wife, how fleeting the experience of love is, how precious it is, how grateful we must be to experience it — and how few people actually experience it, even if just for an instant! Certainly not Pauline, who, despite being married with nine children, cannot recognize our feelings for what they are because she has never experienced such feelings herself.

So we opened M. Bête's *eau de vie* and made a toast to him. Then we had a lovely night and began the next day feeling very sunny for a change.

Your son,

Tim

Mas La Viguerie

Dear Mom and Dad,

I'm quickly knocking out this note to you, so you'll have some sense of what's going on, just in case I don't get a chance to write before all plans are set in motion.

Yesterday, completely out of nowhere, Père Pasquier, the priest who had backed out several weeks ago, called Catherine to say that he was now prepared to marry us.

We're not sure what happened to change his mind, but he said he was willing to perform the ceremony right away. We know that the bishop overseeing Père Pasquier would have had to give his approval, as based on what Josette told us it is unlikely this priest would have acted on his own. So who knows what byzantine machinations led to the reversal, or who intervened on our behalf? Maybe at some point we will find out, but right now we thought we'd better get to that church right away before minds changed again!

We decided that we needed to devise a careful plan. We already have ample evidence of what Pauline and her brood are capable of, and we wanted to make sure that we were not followed to the church. Chicken Lady is now openly spying on us. She shows up early in the morning, her first check-in with us, and then passes by the house at least a half-dozen times during the day. When I caught her near the sheep barn, she just looked at me defiantly and actually threw a rock in my direction. Ah, when love turns to hate.

So we are putting together our own resistance operation. Les Trois Collines is about fifty kilometers from here, in a small medieval village. And, thanks to Count Fishy, we have a cave passage to escape through!

Fishy was thrilled to be enlisted into the maneuver. Actually, we didn't exactly enlist him, we just asked him a question about the cave opening, and he immediately moved to take complete command of Operation Wedding. At first I resisted what I thought was his unbelievable highhandedness. And of course he is unbelievably highhanded. But he was enjoying himself so much that Catherine and I thought it best just to give in. Probably the story of his charmed life.

He turns out to be, however, an extremely competent leader. He called a meeting at the *mas* with his "top lieutenants," a.k.a. Tim and Catherine, and then with detailed maps and timetables he made a presentation that included numbered instructions for all participants. He emphasized over and over the need for precise timing and said that he would not tolerate any foul-ups or there would be hell to pay — and we absolutely believed him.

When it comes to a honeymoon, neither Catherine nor I are sentimental about a strict observation of the ritual, but we do want to get away — more for a rest cure than honeymoon. My mural is turning into a gargantuan enterprise, and I have spent the last two weeks interviewing necessary helpers. Catherine has taken a commission for a painting, plus she has château obligations. So we will go away for about a week, but I'm not allowed to tell you where we're going, because at Count Fishy's insistence the location must be known only to him!

So let's hope all goes according to plan . . . and the gestapo don't ambush us in the road on the way.

Love, Tim

280 West 73d Street, New York

Dear Tim and Catherine,

The photographs of your wedding at Les Trois Collines arrived today. What a charming little chapel, sitting so serenely on top of a hill, with those gorgeous green fields behind. Tim, you of all people know I'm not the weepy type, but as soon as I opened up the package, the floodgates opened too. I think it was the photo of the two of you kneeling side by side on those luscious-looking red velvet prayer stools in front of the altar that really did me in . . . or maybe it was because the photo showed a view from the back and we couldn't see your faces, making the scene all the more poignant: Catherine in such a billowy and enchanting blue gauzy dress and Tim in such an austere black suit, an outfit that never seemed possible before! Your father and I plunked down together on the couch in the living room and devoured all the photos. Hours went by and then finally we had to abandon them and collapse into bed; in the morning we took them up again.

I called Holly to tell her that photos had arrived, and she rushed over with the baby strapped to her front. Tara spat up on some of the snaps, but I don't think it was meant as a comment. Holly was uncharacteristically quiet as she stared at the pictures. *Mute* is probably the best word; she usually instantly sprays thoughts out, but not this time. I got the sense that she was so full of feeling that she was afraid that if she said even one word she would end up overwhelmed.

And what a group of attendees at your ceremony! I think I recognized them all from descriptions in your letters. There was no mistaking the rotund Count Fishy or the prehistoric M. Bête, two really extraordinary-looking people.

And I think another man might be your boatman friend, Paul, and the younger man, Catherine's nephew, Roger?

And then there was Yvette, looking so ethereal. Oh God, that woman breaks your heart. And Josette, so solemn and saintly, looking exactly as I imagined her and then some. I felt such affection for each and every one of them.

Your father had tears in his eyes, a milestone. I think of all that has happened in such a short time, less than three years, and what an amazing story it is. Do I still feel some anxiety? Of course . . . but if I've learned anything from recent events, I know how impossible it is to see into the future. And this will seem even *more* impossible to you: words fail me.

We send love to you both,
Mom and Dad

EPILOGUE

....

JUNE 2005

280 West 73d Street, New York

Dear Tim and Catherine,

Holly *et famille* have been back in New York for at least three weeks since their trip to visit you, and I finally, finally prevailed on her to come by so I could set my eyes on my granddaughter — and of course get the dope on their stay in France. Tara, by the way, is getting more delicious by the day, and your sister thinks I am in danger of seriously overhugging the child, which may be true.

Clearly Tara was entranced by everything at the château and as soon as she arrived she began running around our living room describing how she played hide-and-seek in all the château rooms. There were millions and millions of rooms, Grandma, and Mommy couldn't find me. She found this extremely funny, although it was clear from Holly's face that she gave your sister quite a hard time when they were there with you. When I gave Tara a piece of bread and jelly, she took a bite and then immediately turned her nose up, saying she had had much better jelly at the château! She also kept talking about Aunt Cath-er-een, who she says gave her some gorgeous little clothes for dress-up play that were her own from childhood and perfectly preserved. It was so very thoughtful of her. Please tell her that from me.

Although it was left unspoken, I gather that son-in-law Brad was somewhat less than entranced with his accommodations. Holly says he's not exactly the rugged-traveler type, and now that he has taken up golf, he was astonished not to find a single golf course in the area. I get the impression that there was much tension between them when they were there. I also got the sense that your sister was a bit jealous of what she kept describing as the unbelievable rapport between you two. She says she was always hearing lots of laughter, even at six in the morning. I think she was looking for chinks in the armor of your love . . . not in a mean-spirited way, please don't misunderstand, but in an effort to convince herself that everyone must have the same problems in relating that she and Brad have. She is always moaning to me that she is not getting her "needs met." Whenever I hear her say this — and it is becoming more frequent — it strikes terrible fear in my heart. I really worry for their marriage, as they both seem so immature to me sometimes. And then of course I worry about Tara, who would become just another child of divorce. But enough of that. I don't want to dwell on it.

Holly says that you took them all for a drive to the abbey (sorry, I don't remember the name) to see your murals and that she was extremely impressed by them. What a massive undertaking, she kept saying, and she couldn't stop talking about how disciplined you must have been to deal with all the complexities of the installation. She says there's only one more panel to go.

Oh, I almost forgot: Holly says she actually met the famous Pauline, who showed up one day unannounced, although it was apparently not her time to be at the château. So I gather there is some kind of *détente* now, but Holly says Catherine told her that Pauline likes to break the rules in little ways, just to be a little annoying, when she is now constrained from being a lot annoying. Madame was full of smiles and good cheer, Holly says, and immediately began advising her on the proper way to raise Tara. Some things obviously never change, but they can be redirected, I guess.

Your father and I are looking forward to seeing you both in September.

Lots of love,
Mom